to the keepers of Woodstock's magic

tinker street

A NOVEL

maureen mcneil

Tinker Street

Copyright © 2024 by Maureen McNeil

All rights reserved.

Published by Emperor Books

Bellerose Village, New York

ISBN

Print 978-1-63777-542-4 / 978-1-63777-543-1

Digital 978-1-63777-541-7

Cover photo: Sergio Purtell / cover design: Melanie Roberts

This is a work of fiction. All of the characters, names, incidents, organizations, and dialogue in this novel are either the products of the author's imagination or are used fictitiously.

ONE

"MA," Maggie said. "I'm fifteen on Saturday. Did you get time off so we can do the birthday hike? Carol offered to babysit."

"Yeah," she called from behind the closed bedroom door. "I will today."

Julia was late for her shift at the health food store, where she worked part-time since the store opened in the 1970s. But hearing Maggie call her "Ma" made her feel tender, and she paused in front of the mirror. She remembered herself at fifteen, playing electric piano in her boyfriend's band on Saturday nights; at seventeen, they drove across the country to the Woodstock Festival and never looked back. But time was strange. Maggie grew up so fast at Old Red, a communal house with eight children, three mothers, two fathers, and miscellaneous other adults. Stevie was the oldest kid. Next was Maggie, two years younger. To avoid confusion, the children called their mothers by their first names. Nine years later, when the twins, Mick and Mia, were born, she insisted they call her "Mama." When they turned four, Julia moved the family into town, hoping to slow time.

Saturday was cool and dry, perfect for a hike. Maggie and

Julia noted that new signs had been posted along the two-and-a-half mile hike to the top of Overlook Mountain: *Beware of Rattlesnakes. Stay on the trail.* The mountain was so steep that stepping off the trail in most places meant stepping off a cliff. Loose rocks of various sizes made the switchbacks tricky, even when the ground was dry, and the way down was always treacherous. Last birthday, Maggie wore sneakers and lost both of her big toe nails, which took six months to regrow. Now, they had to watch out for rattlers.

The trail flattened near the top when they reached the ghostly concrete and stone ruins of a 1920's lodge that had burned. From there, Maggie and Julia headed over to the metal fire tower. Four new wooden picnic tables had been installed. They set their backpacks down at the only empty table and took turns swigging from the water bottle.

"Let's climb the fire tower before lunch," Julia said.

The thin handrail and narrow steps always felt rickety. Like a game, they paused at each of the nine landings to take in the widening view of the Hudson River Valley, running north and south. To the west, three lakes nestled like puddles in the greenery of the Catskills. Looking eastward, the Berkshire peaks in Massachusetts were locked in a cloud. Maggie and Julia inhaled the cool, clean air before cautiously heading back down.

Sitting across from each other at the picnic table, nibbling leftover Greek salad and cold pizza, they watched squirrels chase up and down the trees. Julia smiled as three young guys sat down at the other end of their table chatting in Mandarin, and a stranger, wearing loose dun-colored pants and shirt, wandered over and offered the hikers a treat from his paper bag. As he approached, he peered from beneath his knit hat into each person's eyes.

"Thanks," said one of the students. He turned to his friends: "It's pineapple."

"Mine's apricot," said another.

Julia pulled a fig from the bag and thanked him, smiling. Maggie declined the fruit, but offered the man a chocolate cupcake with frosting that Julia had baked. With this, he lifted his hat off his shaved head. Standing tall, without much flesh on his bones, his eyes crinkled like sardines. He bowed his head and returned to the log, where he had left a small backpack. Maggie watched from a distance as he pulled the wrapper off the cupcake and took a bite. She guessed that he came from some far-off culture.

"I can keep a secret," Maggie said. "I want to know my father's name."

Julia looked at her handsome, capable daughter. She saw him in Maggie's eyes, her broad face and tiny nose. Moving the family into town didn't stop the whirlwind and even seemed to speed things up. When the twins' father, John, left for California, Maggie took on the bulk of the childcare: she picked the twins up at kindergarten, cooked their dinner, bathed them, brushed their teeth, and read *Charlotte's Web* aloud four nights a week while Julia's jazz trio performed at local clubs. Maggie also babysat while Julia stocked shelves at the health food store, during the Saturday morning meditation class she taught in their living room, and Sunday afternoons when Julia's three long-time adult students arrived, one after the other, for piano lessons. As Maggie rose to every responsibility her mother presented, Julia reciprocated by supporting Maggie's independence. There were a few exceptions, such as when Maggie dropped out of high school to study for the GED last spring. Even then, Julia did not put her foot down.

"Happy Birthday, Maggie," Julia said. "You've grown up so fast. If I could give you any gift, it would be the art of slowing time."

"Last week, a guy playing guitar on the village green claimed to be my biological father. I said, 'No way! Julia had a virgin birth.' "

Julia covered her mouth and laughed. She leaned in and whispered: "Imagine how Mary must have felt with everyone broadcasting the birth of her baby in the manger."

"And I think of the closed-mouthed Joseph standing by, like my father—it makes me feel sad."

Julia sighed as she removed the paper from the second cupcake. It was her mother's WWII recipe, made with oil rather than butter. The sour milk, baking soda, and cocoa gave it a tangy dark chocolate flavor. After a second bite, she gave the cupcake to Maggie.

"I mean," Maggie continued. "Just how many guys did you sleep with when you were trying to get pregnant with me?"

Julia licked her fingers and took a swig of water. "I had something called endometriosis. It's a thickening of the uterus lining that makes conceiving difficult. It took over three years, so I'm afraid I asked more men than I intended. And for the record, men around town tell *me* that you are their daughter."

Now Maggie sighed. "But if I was their kid, wouldn't they have to pay child support?"

"I never wanted that."

"Not even from my sperm donor? I mean, my father?"

"It wasn't like that with your father, Maggie. We fell in love. We weren't trying to conceive."

"So my birth is really a tragedy because you couldn't live together?"

Julia smiled. The students at the table were packing up. Once they headed back down the trail, she continued: "Maggie, love is never a tragedy."

"So tell me. I want to know."

"Your father is dead," Julia whispered without emotion.

The lie smacked mother and daughter. It constructed a wall

between them, which Julia hoped would put an end to Maggie's needling. A wall was better than the pressure ballooning over them this last year, Julia guessed. Maggie found nothing romantic about a sperm donor for a father or even being a love child, as Julia referred to her. She didn't understand how freedom to have sex with *whomever* had anything to do with love. But being a *real* love child was different. Maggie savored this nugget of information, and turning it over in her head made her glisten.

TWO

STEVIE TAPPED Maggie's bedroom window, calling her name. His voice caught in the lullaby of the Millstream that flowed behind the house. She woke, remembering the lock click on Julia's bedroom door around 1:30, followed by sounds of sex. She wondered if it was the bearded guy or if Julia brought home someone new.

"Maggie!" Stevie pleaded.

This time, she jumped up. Already dressed in sweatpants, socks, and a flannel shirt, she grabbed her coat and tip-toed down the hall. Squeezing through the broken sliding door in the living room, she stepped into her rubber boots on the screened porch. Stevie's old pick-up was parked at the corner, the back end filled with the usual metal scraps. Maggie kissed her friend Carol's cheek as she slid into the cab beside her and buckled her seatbelt. The points of the moon twisted in tree branches as Stevie downshifted on the switchbacks of Ohayo Mountain road. By starlight, Maggie saw prayer flags strung across house porches and the golden dome of the Tibetan Monastery pressed against Overlook Mountain. Where the road took a steep downhill turn, Stevie screeched on the brakes and pulled over at Magic Meadow.

"Give me some words," Carol called.

"Terrific," Maggie shouted. "Radiant. Humble."

Carol sprayed foam across a rock outcropping, writing sideways to fit the letters in among her graffiti. The can empty, she touched a lighter to the foam, and the three jumped back: an incandescent green flame rolled like the Aurora Borealis off the rock until, its fuel spent, they sank back into darkness. A curve of moon lifted above the woods like a winking smiley face with the red planet as its eye. Their laughter sounded like a snarl of coyote pups in an eating frenzy.

Now Stevie shined the truck's headlights across Magic Meadow and set up a large metal ring welded on a stand. He piled heavy rocks on top of the stand and further secured it by twisting wire around the ring and pulling it taut between trees on either side. Maggie and Carol dragged a mattress from the truck and placed it on the downhill slope just beyond the ring. Stevie fetched two buckets of stream water as a precaution. Finally, he screwed his camera to the tripod, moved it back far enough to take in the whole scene, and adjusted its legs for stability.

"So what's it going to be?" Carol asked.

"Put this on." He tossed them each a flame retardant coverall and stepped into a pair of his own. "Tie the hood close to your face. Tuck your hair inside."

Stevie was known at school for his Friday night festooning and welcomed the kids who gathered at the edge of the woods. He learned to juggle oranges when he was ten, and by eleven, he rode around town on a unicycle. In eighth grade, he won first place at the school science fair for an exhibit demonstrating how humans learned to resist gravity and walk upright.

"Rolling," he said and lit the hoop. A thin ring of orange

flame blossomed. He somersaulted through the fire and landed on his feet, raising his arms to Maggie and Carol. Claps erupted from the neighborhood kids at the roadside.

Before focusing, Carol jumped on the balls of her feet and flailed her arms. Her left foot hit the ring as she belly-flopped onto the mattress. Flames frolicked as the hoop swung back and forth. Flush with adrenalin, she hooted and jumped back in line.

Maggie swiped her fingers through the flame, testing it, and feeling no pain, tucked her head. She shot through the hoop like a bullet and rolled into the dewy darkness. Knowing the flame's short life, she hurried up the hill, rubbing a bruised shoulder. They each took a second jump before the fire burned out, leaving them in the stillness of the truck's ghostly headlights.

"I want to watch Philippe Petit practice tightrope walking," said Maggie.

"How about Friday," said Carol. "My morning classes are canceled."

"If it's not raining," Stevie said. "He practices for three hours, so it's a big commitment."

Stevie loaned Maggie *The Thinking Body*, a book Petit suggested he read when the two met at the row of mailboxes at the end of their street. "Actors need to learn how to bring movement into consciousness to control their body and make adjustments," Petit said.

When Friday rolled around, Maggie cleared brush. Carol spread a blanket and set out a bottle of water. They laid on their stomachs in their winter coats a half hour before Petit appeared. As he climbed a ladder to the barn's flat roof, Stevie lifted his binoculars. Petit held his forty-five-pound pole perpendicular to the wire as he stepped out, walking the length between the two barns on the quarter-inch wire. At the second barn, he turned and walked back and then forth, then out and back again six more times.

The three friends had watched the video of Petit's 1974 walk between the World Trade Towers many times and had discussed how his team could possibly sneak eight tons of equipment to the roofs. They marveled at the fact that he had stepped on a nail that very week and proceeded with his daring act anyway, that he talked to the gulls flying beside him and the cops waiting to arrest him. Watching the video, Maggie imagined that Charlotte had climbed to the top of the towers and secretly knit a web of silk with her spinnerets: she would have caught Petit if he fell. But now, observing Petit in person as he knelt and then laid flat on the wire between the barns, it wasn't at all like pulling the curtain back and seeing Oz as a human being: they saw Petit as a god.

The sky was blue, unclouded in every direction, and the temperature sixty-eight degrees the day Stevie, Carol, and Maggie drove to the Trailways Bus Station in Kingston. From there, it was a two-hour bus ride into Manhattan. Maggie watched Stevie and Carol from across the aisle, curled together in sleep like the twins. Breathing with them as their bodies rose and fell, she wondered if they had sex on her living room couch on Friday nights when Stevie slept over. Maggie always went to bed before Carol walked home, and Julia never got back from her gig before 1:00 a.m. Several times a week, Stevie picked Carol up from her private school in Poughkeepsie, and maybe they went to Stevie's house or parked at some dead-end along the Hudson. As Maggie watched the passing landscape from the bus window, she wrote in her notebook: I want a thinking body like Petit; to write and perform like Shakespeare; to love as Stevie loves; to be as compassionate as Carol; to spin silk like Charlotte, strong as iron; and to flap my wings like Mick and Mia.

At the 42nd Street bus terminal, they boarded the downtown E train to Cortlandt Street and followed the signs to the World

Trade Center Plaza. Men and women on their lunch hour hurried past. A tour group paused as their leader waved a small orange flag. In unison, the group pointed upward at the towers and clicked their cameras. A wind tossed Maggie's hair across her face. Scrunching her hands in her pockets, she spied an empty bench and lay down. This was the plan: to focus on the sky where Petit walked. He had forced himself to look down at the plaza so he'd have a memory of it. Now, looking up at that space gave Maggie courage. She had to prepare her mother for her departure. It was happening—improbably, unstoppably— like Charlotte's egg sack ballooning, like a man walking a tightrope 1,368 feet above New York City.

THREE

THE WOODSTOCK TOWN green was a place of vitality, like the old reptilian brain: a place for sleeping, eating, drinking, smooching, and just breathing. Stevie, Carol, and Maggie considered it their home stretch. It's where Stevie got his first kiss in third grade, where he learned to swear, and where, one dark night, he dislocated his hip wrestling two guys from Brooklyn. For Carol, the town green was the place where she staged her plays and collected money for the women's shelter, the place where she drank coffee and sometimes harder stuff. For Maggie, it was her lookout: she searched for a man, tall as she was tall, with broad cheekbones and her signature teardrop nostrils.

On weekends, Maggie painted her face with tiny flowers and wore an old white sailor top with a square collar and white bell-bottom pants. She scanned the passersby, sketching observations in a notebook. It was not only men who approached Maggie with information; various women pulled her aside in stores and at the playground to whisper the minutiae of her birth. Their words, like sticks and stones, piled in her head. She tried to puzzle the facts together, and even though their details didn't add up, these tales made Maggie feel like she belonged: she was part of the big bang, a speck of gold in the expanding universe.

It was during Carol's production of *King Lear in Fourteen Words* that Maggie first felt the presence of a father. She thought posting flyers around town might lure him to the performance. Everyone in town kept their eye out for Maggie, offering rides when they passed her and the twins walking home from kindergarten, to violin lessons, and birthday parties. Surely, someone would mention to her father that she was performing on the town green.

At Stevie's trumpet call, drivers on Tinker Street slowed and stuck their necks out the window as they passed. He wore a gold cardboard crown with LEAR stenciled in black. His three daughters wore their names on bandanas tied around their heads: Carol cast herself as GONERIL; a boy named Django played REGAN; and Maggie was CORDELIA.

"How much do you love me?" LEAR asked his three daughters.

GONERIL and REGAN raised large placards with a hundred hearts drawn in red marker while CORDELIA pointed to the heart painted on the left side of her shirt. Swayed by GONERIL and REGAN's abundance, LEAR kicked CORDELIA off the green.

"No Father!" CORDELIA cried. Her voice carried like a loon in the night, ghostly and sonorous, pausing the audience.

LEAR turned to GONERIL and REGAN. *"Take my castle."*

His two oldest daughters smiled. But when LEAR's back was turned, GONERIL and REGAN kicked him off the green, just as he had CORDELIA.

"I'll save you," CORDELIA cried. She ran back toward LEAR, but it was too late. GONERIL poured pretend drops of poison from a paper cup down REGAN's throat. She then stabbed herself with a sharp point of a cardboard knife. LEAR staggered back onto the green to find his three daughters prostrate on the

ground. He lay beside them and raised a placard with a broken heart.

The audience clapped as Django sang out: *The tricks of patriarchy may stem from a seemingly harmless question, but as Shakespeare demonstrates in King Lear, the play ends in tragedy.* Mingling in the crowd as she jingled the coins in her bandana, Maggie spotted the stranger with the brown clothing from Overlook Mountain across the street in front of the ice cream store. He stood as she approached. He bowed his head, turned, and walked down Tinker Street. Fireworks burst inside her.

Stevie, Carol, and Maggie made grilled cheese sandwiches at Julia's, and when Mick and Mia went down for a nap, the three friends assessed their performance. Carol announced that it brought in more than any other play—seventy-six dollars and forty-three cents. Stevie said they needed a second camera and tripod to make a better video. Maggie stood up with a twirl and faced her best friends. Carol and Stevie waited expectedly. Maggie paused to marvel at Carol, adopted as a baby from China: Carol never whined about her birth story, and Maggie longed to be like her.

"Here is what I have to say about the performance," Maggie finally said. "Shakespeare wrote *King Lear* four hundred years ago. Carol, you wrote your version in fourteen words. Two of those words sum up my life. When I yelled out my line—*No, father*—I didn't include the comma. Essentially, I announced to the village of Woodstock that I have no father. This action has freed me. The search for my father is over."

FOUR

MAGGIE DIDN'T LIKE to chit-chat with parents when she picked Mick and Mia up from kindergarten. Once she had a twin in each hand, she was ready to bolt. But Lucy, their teacher, had been her kindergarten teacher, too, and when Lucy cozied to her, smiling, rocking on her feet, Maggie listened.

"I'm wondering if either Mick or Mia would like a haircut or a pierced ear or something," Lucy whispered. "I'm having a hard time telling them apart. Nothing gender-defining, of course, just something so I know who I'm talking to."

Maggie nodded. "It can be challenging. I'll let Julia know."

"Hey," Lucy continued. "I saw *King Lear*. Good job gutting the patriarchy."

Maggie felt luminous all over again. "Lear's arrogance caused a tragedy. I think that's Shakespeare's message."

"You've developed an actor's voice, Maggie. I could never get a peep out of you in kindergarten."

"Yes, I'm learning to *caw*. I get plenty of practice cleaning bird cages at Beth's bird sanctuary."

Walking home with the twins, a neighbor, David, trotted behind them on the narrow dirt path beside the Millstream, his first grader, Ty, on his back. Maggie learned to think ahead to avoid whining and meltdowns. "I have a surprise for you guys," she told the twins. "I made playdough in three colors, and I'm going to teach you how to weave."

The twins flapped their arms and chirped.

"Any chance for a playdate this afternoon?" David asked, coming up beside Maggie.

She caught his eye. "Hey! Sorry, David. Not today. Maybe next week."

He nodded and jogged ahead.

Julia told Maggie that male attention might look like one thing but always came down to the other. Maggie didn't want to call Julia out, but she knew from living with her that women liked sex, too. Woodstock was the embodiment of peace and love since the 1969 festival, even though its history stretched back a hundred and fifty years with reformers, utopians, intentional communities, and social experimentation. These days, single women like Julia raising children by more than one father was normal. John, Mick and Mia's father, also had a seven-year-old son in California. John showed up in Woodstock every year for a month at Christmas to see the twins and make repairs on the house.

On Wednesdays, Maggie rode her bike down Route 212 to the bird sanctuary. The large porch off Beth's living room held over forty cages on shelves and tables. Others hung from the ceiling. Each cage housed four or five small birds of mixed varieties, and they all chattered as Maggie entered. Holding the lightweight, energetic baby birds was thrilling. She removed the soiled newspaper from the bottom of the cages, swabbed the cage with disinfectant, laid down fresh paper, and attached clean plastic water and food trays.

"We have a new cedar waxwing," Beth said. "The storms coming through make the nests soggy, and they fall apart in the wind. As you can see, we're running out of cages, so I put the waxwing with the baby screech owls, and he seems content."

Maggie studied the cedar waxwing. "He already has a red spot on his wings and a black Zorro mask. What does he eat?"

"Berries," Beth said. "The man who rescued him tried to feed him worms, poor thing. We've got to do a better job educating the community."

"How long before it can be released?"

"Probably two weeks."

"Did the rescuer make a donation?" Maggie asked.

Beth smiled. She was always surprised by Maggie's curiosity, especially her concern about overhead. When Maggie finished cleaning all but the owl cages, the two proceeded together. Beth held the old barred owl on her arm while Maggie cleaned. Its broken leg was nearly mended. Maggie decided the owl's face looked human, like a work of art.

Maggie was paid minimum wage for her part-time jobs. Tuesdays and Thursdays, she took the bus to downtown Kingston to Pilar's studio in an old storefront. Side by side, the two of them hand-sewed up on a scaffold. Pilar had a commission of three nine-foot tapestry-like wall hangings for a new federal building in downtown Albany. Standing or sitting, they pushed and pulled needles with a metallic gold-colored thread through several layers of sheer fabric, talking all the while.

"Do you feel the connection?" Pilar asked. "Women have been hand-stitching since the beginning of the Paleolithic era. That's 30,000 years—shelter, clothes, shoes, sails, books, hats, blankets, flesh. Sewing is older than weaving."

Stevie was intrigued with the artwork when he picked Maggie up. She pointed out the area they had completed sewing in five hours. The stitches sparkled not only gold but blue, red, and green in the streetlight. She likened her labor to that of

Stevie's welding and hammering metal. Her fingers were sore and numb. Sometimes, she pushed the needle too hard, and the eye backed into her thumb, or she stabbed her palm with the point. She sucked the blood away to be sure she didn't bloody the fabric.

FIVE

MAGGIE SEARCHED for Julia in the crowded aisles of the health food store after picking up the twins from their fiddle lesson. Julia's shift was ending: she had a car, and this time of day, the twins were wobbly on their feet. Their music instructor had just informed Maggie that the Sizzling Strings, an old-time fiddle band for kids, had a performance Saturday afternoon at Windham Mountain. Maggie and Julia now had to figure out a ride and costumes for them.

The library was only a ten minute walk from the health food store, and Ms. James, the librarian, was expecting Maggie. Sitting in Ms. James' office for the first time was thrilling. Maggie unzipped her backpack to retrieve photographs of the paintings she hoped to exhibit. Ms. James encouraged this kind of community engagement. Everyone in town loved Ms. James. She looked like a beautiful man.

"This is serious," Ms. James exclaimed as she unwrapped the one twelve-inch square panel Maggie brought in. *Life Magazine* was painted in black letters across the top of the small portrait. "Oh! I recognize this Madonna and child—it's Kate nursing her daughter at the Woodstock Festival!"

"Arthur showed me the magazine cover. I had fun giving her the gold halo."

"How did you get into this?" Ms. James asked. "The small size and deep colors on wood panels make them feel like holy relics."

"Arthur gave me a corner of his studio at Old Red when I was seven and taught me to draw trees and birds. And a couple of years ago my friend Stevie found a hundred of these oak panels at the dump, and they inspired me to paint in the style of the Dutch and Flemish from the Renaissance. Arthur has a collection of art books and a beautifully illustrated Bible, so I've learned all the saints with their miracles and suffering. Do you recognize anyone else?"

"Arthur with various birds. And self-portraits!"

"Those were after Rembrandt. Stevie tied pillows to me and pinned a bedspread around me like a cape. The fancy hats are from a thrift store." Maggie cleared her throat. "So what do you think, any chance for a library exhibit?"

"How many portraits do you have?"

"More than forty."

"Would you be willing to give a public talk? Our grants require public engagement as part of our programming." She opened a large leather book to check her calendar. "We have an opening for the month of June."

"Yay," Maggie said. "I'll give a talk."

Brushing a piece of lint from her suit jacket, Ms. James said, "I'll measure the walls and let you know how many we can hang."

"I can paint the edge of the panels black and tack a small metal loop to the back for hanging. Would that be okay? I don't have money for frames."

The phone rang, and Ms. James gave Maggie a thumbs up. "Maggie Pierce, thank you for sharing your work with me."

Crossing Tinker Street, she entered the bookstore. Her friend Carol's parents were reading from their new book titled *Swimming Around the World.* Joan, her mother, read a section about a hundred-year-old women's swimming club in England that dips in cold ponds year-round. Then Arnie, her father, read a section about Lake Ohrid, a World Heritage Site. "Most lakes slowly die after only 15,000 years by gradually filling in with sediment. Ohrid is over a million years old. It's connected to an underwater stream with its own aquatic ecosystem that keeps it fresh."

A young man raised his hand: "I've read bull sharks live in the shallows of the Amazon. How do you swim with those?"

"Yes," Arnie said. "The locals got in the water with us and showed us what to do. You have to always maintain eye contact with a bull shark. They go for a surprise attack. If you are watching them, they won't hurt you."

A small girl raised her hand: "Did you swim *all the way* around the world?"

Arnie nodded. "We did. But that doesn't mean that we swam in every country. We zig-zagged our way around, mostly the northern hemisphere."

Maggie looked around the bookstore for Carol and Stevie, but neither had shown up. Carol planned to take the bus home from her private school after debate class. Maybe there was traffic on the thruway, but what about Stevie? They were all supposed to have pizza together. Maggie shrugged. She bought a signed copy of Arnie and Joan's book and headed home.

SIX

WHEN NELL from the Woodstock School of Art called to ask Maggie if she would assist with the last two drawing classes for thirty dollars a session, Maggie accepted. She prepped materials, took attendance, and cleaned the studio afterward. If an empty easel presented itself, she was allowed to draw alongside the adults. On the last day, Maggie was struck by a seemingly larger-than-life model: he was on his back with his head turned to the right, left hand on his belly, and his right arm, stretching over his head, covered his face. The pose was familiar, like a sculpture she'd seen in Arthur's book on the Uffizi. She'd seen plenty of men skinny dipping in the local swimming holes, but no nude—male or female—this magnificent. She stared as she moved close, her hands on her hips. She swore he whispered something to her, but she couldn't make it out. When Nell entered to start the class, she whispered in frustration: *"So this is my future?"*

Later that week, Maggie caught a ride with Stevie to Old Red, the communal house where they grew up. His welding studio was in the barn, and most of her paintings were still in Arthur's studio. One by one, she examined the portraits stacked against the wall and divided them into piles. Back against the wall, she found the portrait of her mother she had wrestled with last year and walked it over to the barn to show Stevie. Angling the panel into the light of the one small window, she nudged him.

"What do you think?"

He laid his hammer down and took the painting in his hands. "She looks ecstatic."

Maggie nodded. "More like Rossetti's brown study of Beatrice than Julia, don't you think? Do you see the Grand Canyon cracked open between painter and subject?"

"You and your mom aren't getting along?"

"I talk to the Millstream every night, trying to figure her out. I wish I were going off to college like you and Carol in the fall. Carol told me she got an early acceptance to New York University."

"I'm still waiting to see if I'm going anywhere," Stevie said. He looked again at the portrait of Julia: her eyes closed, her neck long, chin skyward, lips parted, and thick hair like a helmet framing her creamy face. "She's playing the piano, isn't she? It's a love letter to Julia. Give it to her. You'll feel better."

Maggie flopped down in the one folding chair and shut her eyes, posing as her mother posed. "Why is it when you fall in love, you feel pain?"

Stevie shrugged. "The more you love, the more you feel." Returning to the anvil, he swung his hammer. "That guy never called you?" he asked between swings. "Come with us to Fern's party on Saturday. We've got to celebrate your GED exam."

"I won't know if I passed until January."

"You said it was easier than the practice tests."

"Actually, reading, writing, arithmetic, science, social studies —it's kind of a joke. The test to become an American citizen is harder. I memorized all those answers just in case they snuck them in, which would only be fair. But, nope."

SEVEN

THE HOUSE TURNED into a construction site with the twin's father's annual December visit. Thinner and grayer than last year, he still dressed in shorts and hiking boots. He took Julia's to-do list seriously, touring each room with a notebook and tape measure, listing the supplies he needed to purchase. A persistent leak beneath the kitchen sink and replacing the sliding glass door to the screened porch were at the top of John's list, but he also planned to paint the living room, kitchen, hallway, and bathrooms. For Maggie, John's arrival meant a break from babysitting. For Mick and Mia, it meant having a dad for a month. And Julia? A sleeping partner, as they took up where they left off.

Light snow fell the night of Fern's party. Maggie pushed her unruly hair into a black knit cap, like a beehive on top of her head, and painted her face with blue periwinkle, its five petals like tiny windmills. She sewed a short black velvet tunic with a boatneck, leaving holes for her arms and cut fringe at the waist, then pulled on black jeans. Lacing her army boots on the bench at the front door, she watched the twins cuddle with John on the couch in front of the TV. Their faces looked identical as they watched a rented cartoon from the video store, but Mick wore the pointed magician's hat Maggie made out of the black velvet for the Sizzling Strings performance and Mia, the braided wreath of multicolored ribbons that tied around her head and hung down her back like a ponytail. In fact, the twins hadn't taken off their headgear all week, and their teacher, Lucy, gave Maggie a thumbs up. She could tell them apart.

"I'm staying at Carol's tonight," Maggie said, giving each kid a kiss.

"Those painted flowers are magnificent, Maggie," John said. "Vinca minor. Commonly called periwinkle or myrtle, related to the petunia."

Maggie smiled. "You know your flowers."

Fern's parents' sprawling single-story house stood in the middle of an old orchard on Cooper Lake Road. Bobby's band, The Toys, played in the crowded family room. A strobe light seemed to chop the dancers into cubist paintings. Stevie opened three beers, and the friends toasted. Maggie swallowed hard as the peppery bubbles slid down her throat. She had seen The Toys play at a high school dance last year and knew Bobby and his dad, Bruce, from potlucks at Old Red years ago. Now, Bobby was Fern's boyfriend. He was blonde like Kurt Cobain, the heartthrob of the high school girls. Even Maggie held a secret place in her heart for Nirvana's *Unplugged* album.

"Glad you made it, Maggie. I miss seeing you in the halls," Fern said. Every few moments, her hand swished her long brown bangs from her eyes. The rest of her hair was tied up in pigtails. "How's it going?"

Maggie nodded. "I took the GED, so I'm working and saving my pennies."

"That was bold to drop out of school. You're skipping two years; if you pass, you'll be six months ahead of us seniors."

Maggie shrugged. "Where are you going to college?"

"I haven't decided," Fern said. "I don't feel ready to leave Woodstock."

"You'll take the magic with you," Maggie said. "That's what I think. What about Bobby?"

"He's going to one of the California schools. How about you?"

"I'm going to The Metropolitan Museum of Art," Maggie said.

Fern slapped her thigh and laughed.

"College isn't my thing," Maggie said. "Not yet, anyway."

The dining room was set with a long table of food. One couple lingered on a couch, kissing between bites they popped into their mouths with their fingers. Maggie took a plate and selected olives, cubes of parmesan, and a stuffed grape leaf. She sat on the wide hearth of the fireplace, warming her back, when a tall young man sat down beside her.

"Hello, Flowers," he said. "It's Maggie, isn't it?"

She pushed the pit out of her mouth and put it on her plate. "Are you a friend of Fern's?" she asked.

"Yeah, we met in a Bard high school program last summer."

"How'd you know my name?"

"Nell at Woodstock School of Art told me. You whispered something to me about *the future*. I wanted to meet you."

Maggie stood and walked backward. She had not forgotten his marbled pose and, in fact, had borrowed Arthur's book on the Uffizi so she could study it. Still, she wanted to see more, just to be sure. "Can you roll up your sleeve, please?"

"Like this, right?" With one hand on his stomach, the other covered his turned head. "You probably remember more than my arms."

"I remember all of you, except I never saw your face."

Goosebumps rose beneath her black velvet tunic as she examined his deep-set eyes, large straight nose set square in his cheeks, his mauve colored lips. Again, she felt bewitched. Was she falling in love for the second time with the same guy? *How could this be possible,* she wondered. Sitting back down on the hearth, she tried to still her pounding heart by taking a deep breath. Like Stevie taught her, she counted to ten. The young man intuited his effect on her. He thought she might bolt like an animal in the wild, and when she didn't, he pulled her callused, leathery fingers to his lips.

"I hand-sew for an artist in Kingston," Maggie said apologetically. "The needle tattoos me with each stitch. Up on the scaffold, I hold pins in my mouth, sometimes piercing my lips. That really hurts."

"Let me see."

Maggie lifted her chin, flirtatiously puckering her lips. She wanted a kiss but couldn't risk letting him slip away again. "What is your name?"

"Rip," he said.

A broad smile transformed her face, and her whole body relaxed: "As in Winkle?"

"As in Jorgensen."

"Maggie!" Carol called. She and Stevie stood at Fern's front door. When Maggie signaled for them to come into the room, Carol shook her head. "We'll wait for you in the truck."

Maggie flushed. The delicious moment was stumbling by when what she really wanted was time to slow down. Remembering the spell Washington Irving conjured deep in the Catskills, she willed it to happen. She swore the moment lasted at least a decade.

"Rip," she said, trying out his name. It was short and soft. "Rip," she said again, slower. Her mouth opened on the R, lips closed to make the P sound with a puff of air. She stepped into his arms and shut her eyes. And his kiss, round and smooth as polished marble, filled her mouth.

EIGHT

STEVIE AND MAGGIE headed out to Old Red in his truck again, this time to sketch a new portrait of him. The big house was empty as Arthur and Kate, the only remaining commune members who lived there anymore, were visiting friends in Florida. Stevie took off his boots and socks at the door and barefoot, wearing only a T-shirt and jeans, shivered. Maggie tossed him Arthur's old painting sweater. Then, needing better natural light, she set up in the living room and pulled the curtains open. Across Route 212, the frothy Beaverkill Creek crashed down the mountainous bed of boulders. Stevie settled into the lotus position: his bare heels on his thighs, hands together, thumbs crossed. As she began to sketch, she remembered her conversation with Carol about the ancient Buddhist practice of zazen.

"I see the need for zazen," Carol told Maggie. "A core connection or unity that might give you the strength to fix our poor fucked up world. I guess I just didn't meditate enough to get there."

"Is that your plan?" Maggie had asked her. "To fix our poor fucked up world?"

"I want to study Arabic, Chinese, Spanish, history, literature, and playwriting. And join the Peace Corps after college. And study at Oxford—that I've wanted to do since visiting with my parents when I was nine."

Maggie focused again on Stevie and remembered him telling her that he liked the rituals: taking off his shoes at the entrance, dropping a dollar bill into the donation box even though no one was checking, sitting in the dim light on one of the small pillows spaced in a long row. Maggie told Stevie that to her, experiencing the world meant traveling and seeing it for herself. He argued that the real world could also be found within.

"As I work, I sometimes feel the spirit of the stone and wood, even metal," Stevie said. "Zazen is right at your gut, two inches below your belly button."

Maggie's laugh rumbled deep and low like a thunderhead in the distance.

"Study yourself to forget yourself," he continued. "That's the point. To reach stillness is important to being human. It takes a lifetime to perfect."

As if warmed up, Maggie's hand now moved over the paper with quick pencil strokes. From this sketch, she would paint his image on one of the small wooden panels. When she moved back to critique her drawing, she was stymied. Comparing her sketch to others she had tacked on the studio wall, they all had the same ragged curly hair, freckled skin, and long, narrow face. Only today, her picture was not of a boy. She drew a man.

NINE

ARTHUR'S SHOW, *Through the Looking Glass,* opened at the Woodstock Gallery, featuring large paintings of local birds in their natural environments. Even though Maggie had seen the four-foot paintings before, she loved the experiential aspect of his work: viewers were required to search the swamp marsh to find the heron, or an owl camouflaged as tree bark, or a common robin the size of a cat hidden in a pine bow. This last painting had a red sticker next to it. Maggie had begged Beth to come to see Arthur's paintings as they both loved birds and to Maggie's delight, Beth appeared at the gallery door.

"Maggie," Beth said, "I didn't recognize you. What are you wearing?"

"I dress up in uniforms when I go out. I buy them used at the Army Navy store. This is a postal service uniform."

"And the tattoos?"

"It's paint. I paint flowers on my face for special occasions. Come look at Arthur's robin over here. See its brown eyes flecked with yellow? If you look carefully, Arthur painted the Tree of Knowledge in its iris. He makes the viewer use their eagle eyes to fully see his pictures."

"Beautiful," Beth said, standing on tip-toes.

Arthur joined them, dressed in black jeans, a white shirt, and a red baseball cap.

"Beth, this is my friend, Arthur," Maggie said.

Beth held out her hand. "Beautiful work. My birds are all in cages. I need to get out into nature more often."

Arthur's mouth moved before he gave his words sound. "I think we've met before," he finally said. "Maggie's been telling me about the bird sanctuary. Do you have any owls right now?"

"Yes, I have an old barred owl recovering from a broken wing. It's mating season, and he hoots all night long. Inside the house, it's very loud. He keeps me awake."

"He is so pretty," Maggie said. "He's got those dark eyebrows and those striped brown and white feathers."

"Would it be possible for me to come over and make some sketches?"

She gave him her card. "I'll release him in about two weeks. Just give me a call."

Maggie and Stevie left for the coffee shop as soon as he gave Arthur a hug. She hadn't seen Stevie since a picnic table fell on Lefty's leg when the two of them tried lifting it into the truck. Lefty was recuperating after surgery but was housebound in their small cabin with forty steps up to the front door.

"How's he doing?" Maggie asked.

"He's miserable. I have to bathe him and shop and cook and clean up."

"It sounds like taking care of the twins," Maggie said. "I could cook and clean and hang out with him on Wednesday while you are at school if you don't mind picking me up and taking me home."

"Are you going to get your driver's permit, Maggie?"

She shook her head. "I'm not buying a car, so it wouldn't help me to get around."

"Rip hasn't called you since the party?"

She looked at him over her coffee cup. "I got his contact info from Fern."

"Fern says he's the star of the Rhinebeck tennis team. He's got a busy schedule. But he's not going to forget you, Maggie. Nobody ever forgets you."

"Do you want to drive by his house? I'll give you five bucks for gas."

It was Thursday, a week before Christmas, and the shops in the center of Rhinebeck were decorated with wreaths and lights. Turning onto Rip's street, they found number 68, a stone house two blocks off Main. It was one of several early, well-cared-for stone houses in town. Stevie made a U-turn and parked across the street. His rusty truck was distinctive and certainly out of place. Parked in the driveway was a Honda. The house lights were on, but they saw no one.

"Falling in love is a physical thing, isn't it? It's not rational. It's like that time we ate magic mushrooms, and we just had to wait for them to wear off."

"Don't be so hard on yourself. Think of it as a love bite, a taste of bliss to come."

"Like Dracula? Do I get to live forever?"

Stevie laughed.

"It's not funny, Stevie. I really want Rip to climb in through my window and steal me away. It sounds horrible, like some trashy novel."

He pretended to twist her nose like he used to do when they were little, but Rip's screen door banged closed, and they turned their attention to the house. A big yellow Labrador with a wagging tail seemed to be walking a man with a hat down the driveway, possibly Rip's dad. At the end of the driveway, they crossed the street and moseyed toward Stevie's truck. At the telephone pole, right in front of them, the dog paused, sniffed, and lifted his leg. As if to give the dog privacy, the man turned his eyes toward the truck. Maggie felt his gaze and sank down into the seat.

"Satisfied?" Stevie asked when the man and dog had passed.

"It's not what I was hoping for, but at least I saw Rip's dog pee. I guess we can go home now."

TEN

A LETTER from the Department of Education arrived on Christmas Eve, congratulating Anna Magdalena Pierce on passing her GED exam. Maggie stuck the letter with a safety pin and hung it on the family Christmas tree. Keeping the news to herself, even for five minutes, made her feel nauseous. She called Stevie and then Carol to let them know. Restless, she walked through town lit with holiday lights and gazed into store windows as the last few shoppers made purchases. John and Julia's Christmas gift to Maggie was a Macintosh computer, which John had already installed in her bedroom. Maggie's gifts to the family were wrapped under the tree: two small paintings of dogs, one for each of the twins; Maggie's Beatrice portrait for Julia; and for John, a drawing of the twins from last year, asleep on the living room floor. Also under the tree was a hand-sewn cloth book for Carol of her play, *King Lear in Fourteen Words*, with stick figures and words stamped in inky comic-style bubbles. For Stevie, she had a charcoal drawing of his father, Lefty, that she made when she was twelve. Convinced that she would never hear from Rip, she had sent him the sketch she drew of him at The Woodstock School of Art and added a stick figure of herself with her hands on her hips, gazing at him. In a bubble, she wrote: *So this is my future?* The pain of his rejection ebbed a little each day. She was proud when her feet settled on the ground, even if the memory of his kiss remained in her mouth.

John cooked spicy fried polenta with tomato sauce, a favorite of Mick and Mia's. After dinner, presents were opened. As Stevie predicted, Maggie's gift stitched the wound between mother and daughter: Julia got emotional, embraced Maggie, and didn't want to let go. All five family members were down on the floor, building a Lego castle, when the doorbell rang.

"Hi, I'm Rip. A friend of Maggie's. Is she home?"

"Come in. I'm Julia, her mother."

"I hope I'm not interrupting," he said.

"Welcome, Rip," John said, holding out his hand. "Rip, like Rip Torn. I've always loved that name. The juxtaposition of two synonyms: one present and one past. Like… *Leap Sprung* or *Drop Fell.* Nice to meet you."

Mick poked Rip's arm. "This is the tower where the bad king keeps people locked up."

"I'm making a park with trees for my giraffe," said Mia.

Maggie's mouth hung open in shock. The rest of the room dropped away as Rip sat on the floor beside her. He stuck his finger in her open mouth. When Julia returned to the living room with cups of tea, Maggie licked her lips, listening to Rip answer Julia's questions: he was named after his great grandfather; he came from an old Hudson Valley family; he was on the tennis team at Rhinebeck High School and would soon head to Brown University in the fall.

Finally, Rip turned to Maggie: "My mother wants to meet you. She asked me to invite you to her opening in Hudson the second Saturday in January. Afterward, I'll take you to dinner."

"How does your mother know Maggie?" Julia asked.

"She saw a drawing Maggie sent me," he said. "Her friend

Nell teaches the drawing class Maggie assisted with at the Woodstock School of Art. That's where we met."

"I'm friends with Nell, too. What kind of artist is your mother?" Julia continued.

"A sculptor. She teaches at Bard."

When the twins began to whine for their Disney video, Julia inserted it into the machine and turned down the lights. Maggie and Rip excused themselves and took their tea down the hall to her room. He paused at her mirror surrounded by small lights, her cup with brushes, tubes of paint, and the thick open photobook of colorful flowers. Scanning the wall, he recognized the blue periwinkle from Fern's party.

"You save your flowers?"

"Usually," she said. "Each flower is painted on a foundation of agar-agar, an algae powder I mix with water. It's a strong, elastic-like substance that breathes when it dries. It peels right off with water."

Rip laid his hand on the Macintosh computer. "Nice," he said, continuing toward the window. Teasingly, he pushed the window open, cupped his ear to the Millstream, and smiled back at her.

"You heard that I talk to the Millstream?" she said. "News travels like a burning barn in Woodstock."

"You passed your GED exam! Congratulations! I had to stop by. I hope it wasn't too awkward. Your family seems cool." He leaned in with a kiss like the first time, shockingly round and smooth. "What will you do with yourself now that you have officially completed high school?"

She scooted back on the bed and leaned against the wall. "I'm moving to the city in the fall. Maybe I'll travel a bit first. But at the moment, I'm hankering to know what you said to me that day at the Woodstock School of Art."

"Pose for me."

"Really?" She laughed. "Do you draw?"

He shook his head. "I'm not an artist."

"Okay," she said, unsnapping her flannel shirt. "How about Matisse's *Odalisque*?" She bared her breasts, slid her sweatpants down two inches below her belly button, and with a jubilant stare, she bent her right leg and placed her hands behind her head.

"Beautiful," he said. "How about Ingres' *Odalisque*?"

"I don't know that one."

He pulled off her sweatpants and socks and said, "Take your shirt off and turn toward the wall so I can see your spine. Yep. Up on your elbow. Now turn your head and look at me." He gently bent her legs, pulling the lower one over the other to reveal the bottoms of both feet. "Now, a hand on your ankle." Rip wound her shirt on her head as a scarf. Flicking off the overhead light, he focused the desk lamp on her face and adjusted her head to show her profile. "That's it."

They remained still, smiles frozen on their faces. Finally, he asked: "What would you like?"

She opened the drawer of the side table next to the bed and held up a shiny little packet. "I'd like to know how you feel inside me."

As the Disney soundtrack blasted from the living room, he discarded his clothes, applied the condom, and switched off the light. Their bodies entwined and folded architecturally into a private world of flesh, nerve, and emotion. It reminded her of the two garter snakes she had seen once, cheek to cheek, at the doorstep of Old Red. They held each other until the sound of the car filled with magic candy canes exploded as it neared the North Pole, signaling the end of the movie. After dressing, Rip leaned down to kiss her one last time and let himself out the front door.

ELEVEN

WIND ROCKED Stevie's truck as it sped past grimy snow piled at the edge of Route 28. The forty wooden steps up to Lefty's cabin were scraped and salted but still slick as Maggie ascended. Opening the door, a buttery stream of sunlight fell across the living room, warmed by a wood stove. Lefty rested in the crack of the couch. Up close, Maggie saw that his ponytail was buzzed, his dimples hidden in a round silver beard.

"Hello," Lefty said. "There's coffee in the pot Stevie made. It's probably still warm."

"I'm good," she said, unzipping her coat. "I brought you a thermos of vegetable soup—Kate's recipe, your favorite. Ginger, garlic, mushrooms, scallions, fennel, and ramen."

Maggie squirted soap onto the sponge, ran hot water, and started in on the tippy pile of crusty dishes, pots, and pans in the sink. She laid down a towel and let the clean dishes drip dry on the counter like they did at Old Red. Moving on, she wiped down the table, stove, refrigerator, and toaster and swept the floor. She folded the kitchen towel and, settling into a chair across from Lefty, took out her sketchbook. A sweet, nurturing feeling emanated from him. He had always been there to tie her shoes and comb her hair when she was little. Lefty was the grown-up who read the bedtime story, and even today, he was the one adult in Woodstock Maggie knew would never gossip or misjudge her. When he asked her about "the young man across the river," she didn't hesitate to open up.

"I feel reckless. I've only seen him three times, and I asked him to sleep with me."

"It's good to pick the one you want. Better than letting the guy pick you. Just be safe. Always use a condom."

"I think you'll like him. I asked him to run away with me, but he's very responsible. He plays tennis and is going to Brown in the fall."

"Don't worry about forever. Just enjoy, Maggie. Loving someone is the best feeling in the world."

After he took his crutches to the bathroom to pee, he laid down on his bed and fell asleep. Maggie finished the final touches on the background of her sketch and got up to put the dishes away. Out the window, five or six white goats huddled in the pen, searching beneath the snow for something to eat. Stevie's old red truck pulled up, and she folded the towel and looked to Lefty, sorry she couldn't say goodbye.

"Are you going home?" Stevie asked.

"I'm going to Pilar's studio in Kingston, but if you take me to town, I can catch the bus."

"I'll drive you."

"Thanks, Stevie." They settled into a quiet ride. Stevie wasn't much of a talker usually, and the silence between them was comfortable. But she gave him the rundown of her morning with Lefty. "He's doing okay," she said. "He was tired. He didn't want the soup I brought. It'll be good for dinner. Are you playing chess and music with him? Has he been out to see his goats? You don't want to let him slip into a depression. Remember how awful it was when Julia broke her ankle that winter she was on tour in Europe? Even with all the help at Old Red, she got depressed. And it took months to pay up on all our bills. Maybe you should see if he can start physical therapy sooner rather than later."

Stevie pulled out his sandwich when he stopped to let Maggie out of the truck. She waved as he turned into traffic and headed back to school. As soon as her key was in the door, Pilar called out to her from the top of the scaffold.

"Hi, Maggie. I'm glad you're here," Pilar yelled. "We're right on schedule for the installation. I never could have done this without you, Maggie. We might be able to finish this last section today. If you want to continue working another month or so, I have old theater costumes in the closet that need mending. Let's take a look before you leave."

"I'm taking the 4:10 bus home."

"Alright. Let's see where we are at 3:30. We can go through the costumes another day if we're not done."

Maggie nodded. Before threading her first needle, she pulled out a small camera and took a bunch of close-ups of the work and of Pilar sewing, her nose right up against the fabric. It looked like a beautiful blue sea teaming with life. She would miss this time spent with Pilar. They'd been sewing the tapestry-like wall hangings by hand for months. "I look forward to seeing this hanging in Albany," she said, putting down the camera.

"I'll invite you to the ribbon-cutting ceremony. I don't know the exact date yet."

"What are you working on next?" Maggie asked.

"I'm taking a little break to visit my mother in Mexico. Ever been? You'd love Frida Kahlo and Diego Rivera's studio. Even the zoo is worth going to in Mexico City. The monkeys are so lively and entertaining, they don't seem to know they're in a cage."

That night, around midnight, Carol knocked on Maggie's

window. She unlocked the porch door for her and took Carol by the hand. Wrapped in a blanket on the couch, Maggie caught Carol's tears with her finger. She'd come over in the night once before when Carol first met Stevie. She and her mother had argued because Carol wanted to transfer to the public high school, and her mother wouldn't let her.

"Shall I make you a bed on the couch like I do for Stevie?"

Carol shook her head.

"Want some tea?"

Carol's swollen eyes were nearly hidden beneath her straight dark hair streaked silver-blonde, like the cedar waxwing at the bird sanctuary. Carol was shaken. Maggie knew that birds always felt better around other birds, even different types of birds, especially when stormy weather destroyed their nest.

"I'm six weeks pregnant," Carol said. "I made an appointment for an abortion at a clinic in Kingston. Will you come with me?"

"Of course. When?"

"It's Friday at 11:00."

"Does Stevie know?"

Carol sucked on her lower lip and nodded. "He is giving us a ride there Friday morning. But it's not his. We decided a couple of months ago to date other people."

"Wow, I didn't know," Maggie said quietly. She was confused, even hurt that neither of her best friends had told her they broke up. "What about birth control?"

"I found the condom in the bed, unused—he must have taken it off. The school nurse said boys do that sometimes. I had an HIV test at my mom's insistence. Luckily, it was negative."

When Friday came around, Maggie didn't know quite what to expect and packed a book to read in the waiting room. The clinic was inside a corporate-looking brick building with lots of professional offices. All was quiet in the waiting room except for the occasional babble of a toddler or the hungry cry of an infant in a stroller. Women of various ages, shapes, and colors slouched in their chairs or held hands with their friends or significant others. Now that the procedure was imminent, Carol had regained her usual self-confidence. She chatted about living in the city, her dorm room at NYU, and the incredible internships available. When Carol was taken into the back and prepped on a table, Maggie took out *Pride and Prejudice*, the comfort book she reread every year. But as she thought about the story now, the attitude of Mr. Bennett troubled her. Yes, he was the preferred parent because he didn't push his daughters to marry like their mother, but neither did he seem to care that his wife and daughters would lose their home when he died.

When Carol walked awkwardly into the waiting area with a fat pad between her legs, Maggie used the phone at the desk to call Carol's mother, Joan, for a ride. They took the elevator to the lobby and settled into comfortable chairs. They held hands and stared at the driveway where cars pulled up to the front door.

"Hi, girls," Joan said as Carol eased into the front passenger seat. Maggie climbed into the back, thinking about how sad Stevie must be without Carol. Lefty, too, loved Carol like a daughter. Carol sometimes stayed with them when her parents traveled for research and even had her own room at the cabin. Lefty must have known about Stevie and Carol's breakup. It was his way not to mention it to her.

"I'm proud of you, Carol," said her mother. "We are lucky. It wasn't safe or legal when I was growing up."

Joan had her own story, but now wasn't the time to tell it. Periods, birth control, pregnancy, rape, abortion. These were the things teenage girls often navigated alone. At least Julia had done a fair job informing Maggie about menstruation. She called it basic plumbing. Plumbing with a tragic man-made twist: that girls would always shoulder the blame if anything went wrong.

TWELVE

RIP'S mother's solo show on Warren Street in Hudson was packed. Maggie and Rip wove their way through clusters of people in the main room hand in hand, pausing at the abstract stone and wood sculptures smoothed with hollows. Some sides of the wood looked as if it grew out of the stone; sometimes, the edges were rugged, like they were pulled from an old foundation. Maggie studied Gertrude's drawings next to each sculpture as the crowd crawled by. She and Rip decided to find each other in twenty minutes.

Gertrude spotted Rip and Maggie when they walked through the door and now couldn't take her eyes off Maggie as she navigated the hot, stuffy gallery. Maggie's long coat was open, exposing her Lady Macbeth dress, a dress Pilar had given to her from the costume closet, calling it beyond repair. Cutting it apart, Maggie remade it into a black and silver knee-length confection, keeping the puckered low-cut bodice that pushed her small breasts upward when laced. The long, puffy sleeves had to be taken in when she tried it on with her coat. Tiny white snowdrop flowers, like bells with each petal ending in a point, were painted across the almost non-existent bridge of her nose and wide cheeks. Her dark curly hair fanned like a crown from a twist of red cloth tied around her head.

"How do you do, Maggie? I'm Gertrude, Rip's mother." Gertrude extended her hand. She wore sleek, black textured pants and a turtleneck sweater. Her nose was thin and pointed, her hair short and spiked. "Thank you for coming."

"Nice to meet you," Maggie said, looking around. She placed her chapped hand in Gertrude's. "Your drawings and sculpture pair so perfectly—like innards pulled from bones."

Gertrude nodded. "Nicely put. Rip tells me you have a show of portraits coming up at the Woodstock Library in June. I'd love to see them."

"Yes, I'll send you an invitation. They're only twelve-inch square, so I guess I'm a miniaturist at the moment."

Gertrude locked arms with Maggie, and together, they swooped through the main room into smaller back rooms in order to procure refreshments. Gertrude kept a firm grip on Maggie as they passed Rip, who was knotted in a corner with several athletic-looking young men. And they passed Nell, from the Woodstock School of Art, engaged in a heated conversation with a little wizened man. Then, standing before her was the man she and Stevie had seen walking the yellow lab in front of Rip's house.

"This is my husband, Roland, Rip's stepfather," Gertrude said. "He's an architect, which is what I would be if I had passed my structures class."

Maggie's head dipped as she smiled. She hoped he wouldn't recall the dark night their eyes briefly met through the windshield of Stevie's truck.

"I want you to meet Lulu, a classmate of mine from Rhode Island School of Design," Gertrude said."Lulu, this is Maggie Pierce from Woodstock." Their hands clasped warmly as Gertrude continued: "Lulu has a fabulous contemporary women's art collection. One day, I will take you to visit her, and we'll look at it together.

"Lovely to meet you," Lulu said, flipping her straight blond hair behind her shoulders. "You are wearing my favorite flower! How timely. I saw snowdrops blooming in Central Park just this week!"

"Maggie has a show at the Woodstock Library in June," said Gertrude. "Let's plan to attend."

"I'll send you an invitation," Maggie said, accepting Lulu's card.

Rip's hand reached into the small circle for Maggie and swooped her away. Buttoning her coat as they stepped out into the cold, a wind brushed them sideways. They crossed Warren Street and hurried along Seventh Street to Governor's Tavern. It was the only other lively establishment this cold January night. Inside, a boisterous crowd enjoyed beer and simple fare. They sat across from the bar, facing the front windows. Behind them was a large black and white mural-size photo with the words *Warren Street, 1870* written in black script.

A fast-moving waiter placed menus on their table and held his pen to his pad. They got the message and quickly ordered. Before they knew it, two bowls of chicken soup were delivered to the table, along with a salad for Maggie and a sandwich and fries for Rip.

"*Nobody's Fool* was shot here last year with Paul Newman," Rip said. "Did you see it?"

"No," Maggie said, blowing on a spoonful of soup. Rip seemed taller, sitting across from her. She was used to dining with the twins.

"We'll have to see it," he said. He waited for Maggie to speak, but she continued to take him in. "So what do you say?"

"Your mother's work is intriguing. She's gracious. You're very lucky."

"It's always been easy between us."

"How about your stepfather?"

"Roland is kind and generous. Even-tempered. My father died when I was four."

"So we're both fatherless!" she said. "What happened to yours?"

"A shear microburst blew Pan AM flight 759 out of the air. All 145 on board were killed. I was only four."

"I'm so sorry."

"Because he was a journalist, I've been able to go back and read everything he published, so I know a little bit about him. Unfortunately, I don't have siblings—I never played like you and the twins. I think I've always been a grown-up."

"My childhood is a bit skewed, too, as I've been my mother's partner in child-rearing. I suppose in the olden days, it was nothing unusual."

His eyes grew lively. "Like Willa Cather's *Antonia*. I love that novel."

"Right," Maggie said. "Only Julia pays me."

As they ate their meal, Maggie watched with curiosity as cans of beer were delivered to customers along with their bills. Then she noticed their waiter filling cans from a tap at the bar. She thought it was unusual, but she had no tavern experience, so she wasn't sure.

"I have news," Maggie said. "Julia is moving to California."

"Really? When is this happening?"

She shrugged. "John, Mick and Mia's father, put the house up for sale. He's invited all of us to live with him and his son in Marin County."

"You, too?"

"I'm not going, but potential buyers will start traipsing through our little house very soon. Life as I know it is shifting beneath my feet."

"It could be an opportunity."

"Julia is upset, but in reality, she knows she can't expect me to tag along. Kissing the twins goodbye will be the hard part. And figuring out how to support myself."

"What about your father? Can he help you with living expenses?"

She shook her head without lifting her chin.

"Okay. I won't ask more about *that*!" he said. "What would your ideal situation look like? Earlier, you mentioned moving to the city or traveling."

"If I could have anything, I'd pick an old-fashioned apprenticeship in the city, which includes room and board and a stipend. Something safe so I won't end up living in Central Park."

"That won't happen."

"Tell me about Brown," she said.

"It's where I always assumed I'd go to college. It's where my parents met and where they met Roland. I've attended the annual fundraisers and class reunions since I was little, so I know it well. It'll be fine. In the meantime, why don't you move in with me, Gertie, and Rollie? I'm sure they'd be accommodating."

"That's sweet, Rip, but I couldn't," Maggie said. "I have a handful of adults in Woodstock who will take me in, including Carol's parents. By the way, Carol and Stevie broke up, and neither of them told me!" Maggie sighed. She finished her soup before continuing. "Carol will be at NYU in the fall, so I'll have her nearby. And thanks to her, I've stopped whining about being a 'love child' and not having a father."

"What do you mean?"

"Carol was adopted as a baby from China. She's incredibly accepting and grateful, like you—not a rebel like me." Maggie hesitated. "Imagine what a letdown men will be after knowing you, Rip. I wish we had met in our thirties."

"No way. I'll be conventional and loathsome by then. You wouldn't love me."

The waiter seemed to be in a rush. Even before finishing their meal, a large slice of dark chocolate layer cake with buttercream frosting and two forks appeared at their table. The spritely waiter grinned. "On the house."

"Thanks," Maggie said.

"Thank you very much," chimed Rip.

Maggie took the first bite of cake and sucked the frosting off the fork. "But you are in charge of forming your own character, Rip," she said sternly.

"Repeat after me," he said. *"We will always be here for each other."*

As Maggie wiped a tear away, the old brick building started to rumble and quake. She grabbed his hand. A screeching noise overpowered the diners. Silverware bounced off the tables and onto the floor. A single light shined across the walls, and a two-story high train engine chugged up the street, only a few feet away from the rattling plate glass window. Rip and Maggie ducked under the table as they learned to do during school emergencies, suppressing nervous laughter. When the rattle quieted to a vibration, they lifted the tablecloth. The train engine had come to a halt in front of the tavern. As they climbed back into their chairs, the engineer jumped off the idling monster. They watched in awe as he pushed through the door and sat at the bar, and their sweetheart old waiter poured him a cup of coffee!

THIRTEEN

NEWS SPREAD on Tinker Street that John's house was for sale and that Maggie would not be joining Julia and the twins in California. She subsequently received several offers of room and board for the summer: Miriam over at the high school, whose daughter was leaving for college; Arthur and Kate at Old Red; Carol's parents, the closest and most natural home away from home; Beth at the bird sanctuary; even Rabbi Leon's wife Rosie called to offer her room and board in exchange for babysitting and light house cleaning. And Ms. James, the librarian, said she had an empty apartment above the stable Maggie could move into in exchange for mucking out the barn once a day. Still, other offers dribbled in from parents standing in the schoolyard as she waited to pick up Mick and Mia.

"What about the 3Ms?" Maggie asked Julia.

"I have to find a new bass guitarist for California gigs. I'll figure it out."

"I'm glad for you and John and the twins, but I'll miss you," Maggie said. As usual, the depth of their feelings wasn't articulated, but the impending separation swirled around them. The long, warm Christmas hug was rare. Tip-toeing and sidestepping were their norm. Each was independent in so many ways, yet they both relied on respect and cooperation. Maggie had earned hers, and Julia honored it.

A second morning at the bird sanctuary was added to Maggie's schedule, which now totaled eight hours a week at minimum wage. Maggie approached her mother's friend, Teresa, owner of the bookstore, and asked for a job shelving books. Once she proved herself, she said, she'd like to learn the cash register. Maggie was thinking of all those small stores in Manhattan: if she had some experience, she could always find temporary work once she turned sixteen.

Meanwhile, Maggie did what she could to help prepare for the move. Mick and Mia dressed and undressed as Maggie pulled clothes from their closet. She made snap decisions about which to give away, which to keep, and which to turn into rags. The doorbell interrupted the rhythm. Mick ran to the front door and brought David and Ty into the bedroom. Stepping over the piles of clothes, David plopped down on the desk chair to watch. When the kids started yelling and tossing clothes, Maggie gave up.

"How about some popcorn? And David, would you like a cup of green tea?"

"I thought you'd never ask," he said.

David's drop-in playdates occurred because Maggie always said they were busy when he tried to plan one. His treatment of her vacillated between adult and child, even as she felt consistently in charge. She wanted to complain, but discussing their "relationship" was pointless. The play-dates would soon be coming to an end.

"What's John asking for the house?" David said.

"I don't know. Are you interested in buying it?"

"I enjoyed renovating my house, and this is its twin—I'd love to take another shot at it. Mind if I take a stroll through?"

"Go ahead," Maggie said. As he disappeared down the hall, she yelled. "You should give the realtor a call."

Pouring boiling water through a woven strainer of green tea leaves, she felt again the shock of David squeezing her butt last summer in the Millstream when they were playing with the kids. She dove underwater and, coming up on the other side of the swimming hole, yelled that she had earned a brown belt in tae kwon do in sixth grade in case he had forgotten. He apologized, mumbling that it was an accident.

"What are you going to do in California?" he asked.

Maggie shook salt over the popcorn and took the bowl into the living room. Mia was asleep on the couch. Mick and Ky were on the floor with small trucks, their heads slumped in their arms, yet they all rose to the warm smell.

"I'm moving to New York City in the fall," she said, walking back into the kitchen.

"In that case, if I buy the house, you can live here until September."

Maggie stirred her tea and took a sip. "I'm looking for a live/work situation for the summer so I can save money."

"You could work for me."

She folded her arms over the tabletop and shook her head. "That's not a good idea, David, and you know it."

His face reddened as he was forced to remember her disgust for him that day in the Millstream.

Carol had an interview for a volunteer position with a social justice organization, and Maggie joined her for the day trip to the city. While Carol was busy downtown, Maggie took the uptown C train and got off at 72nd Street. It was early March. Chilly gusts blew budding tree limbs around like helicopter blades. Passing through John Lennon's *Imagine* in Central Park, a guitarist played "Give Peace a Chance." Maggie felt exuberant and carefree. Beyond the big fountain and the rowboat pond, she crossed the road to her favorite Alice in Wonderland statue that she and Stevie had climbed when Lefty brought them to the city. Today, three women chatted on benches as their little charges napped in baby buggies.

Contemplating her Library talk, Maggie headed into the Dutch and Flemish portraits at the Metropolitan Museum. She remembered seeing her first Hans Holbein portrait and being stunned by his dark greens and blues and his small touches of red and the serious white collars and ornate tidbits detailing the model's clothing. In the Greek and Roman section on the ground floor, a marble carving of the *Three Graces* captivated her. She walked around it as if arm-in-arm with them, turning front to back. When none of the male torsos spoke to her, she fantasized about hopping on a plane to Florence to visit the Uffizi in person. In the museum store, she found a book similar to Arthur's and read a portion on Mannerism, the followers of Michelangelo, Leonardo, and Raphael, who used distortion to express emotions. She was entranced by the pictures of the *Sleeping Hermaphroditus* by Bernini, Michelangelo's *Lying Man,* and *Judith Slaying Holofernes* by Artemisia Gentileschi. With only twenty minutes left before she had to catch the subway to meet Carol, she climbed the stairs to the second floor again and sat in front of Caravaggio's *The Denial of St. Peter,* which she had passed by earlier. The trio—soldier, woman, and St. Peter— reminded her of her own trio with Stevie and Carol. Now, Stevie dated Fern, and she was in love with Rip. On the bus ride into the city that morning, Carol informed her she was dating a woman, the editor of the school literary magazine.

"What's sex with a woman like?" Maggie asked.

"Trusting," Carol said. "I like not worrying about getting pregnant."

Maggie got a seat on the downtown 5 train and took out her notebook and pen. She dreamily mapped out a European art tour: Paris, Amsterdam, Madrid, Rome, Florence, and Athens. Then she scratched it out and made a realistic list of New York City cultural institutions she intended to visit.

It wasn't until a couple of weeks later that Stevie met up with Maggie on the town green, carrying two cups of coffee. With the family's move quickly falling into place, they had a lot to catch up on. She explained her intention to use her real name—Anna Magdalena—in the fall.

"Don't count on me calling you anything but Maggie," Stevie said. "You'll always be Maggie to me."

"That's okay. Julia won't call me Anna Magdalena either, and she's the one who named me after Anna Magdalena Bach."

"Is she pissed you aren't going with her?" he said.

"She knows I can't nanny the twins forever."

"Maybe that's why she's moving in with John, to give you a break."

Maggie shrugged. "I'm going to miss my two little birds."

"Let's plan a camping trip into Woodland Valley with Mick and Mia. I always wanted to do that," Stevie said. "When are they leaving town?"

"As soon as the house sells," Maggie sighed.

"We don't have to hike far. The trail is steep to start, but a quarter mile in, there's a beautiful flat campsite. We can set up a tent and tell stories around the campfire after dinner. I want them to remember the Catskills. Would you mind if I ask Fern to come along?"

"Of course not, ask her. But we'll need two tents then."

"I have tents, sleeping bags, and cooking utensils. You plan a dinner and breakfast menu and buy the food. I'll do the rest."

She patted his knee in agreement as they sipped their coffee. Maggie savored the still moments between them. Silence seemed like their own private language. Even if their thoughts or observations of the people around them were not the same, they enjoyed their parallel universe.

Then Stevie broke the silence. "Lefty's been diagnosed with lung cancer."

"No! Lefty has a broken leg!"

"Fern and I are planning to start at New Paltz in the fall, so we can be close by. Surgery is scheduled for next week to remove his left lung."

"Shit! I'm so sorry!"

"He smoked a pack a day from age thirteen. That's thirty years of smoking."

"Let me know what I can do to help."

"I'm staying with Fern's cousin in the city while he's in the hospital. Get your license, and you can use my truck. You already know how to drive—Arthur taught us both when I was fourteen. You were only twelve."

Maggie smiled: "My legs were long enough to reach the pedals. But Stevie, getting my permit isn't going to help much. I can't get my license until my sixteenth birthday."

"That's only a month away. It would give me peace of mind to know you could borrow a car and visit Lefty this summer. He's going to have doctor appointments long term. He'd hate to have to move into town."

FOURTEEN

SANDWICHED on the bleachers between Roland and Gertrude, Maggie watched her first tennis match. She caught Rip looking her way before a serve and hoped she wasn't a distraction. Then again, he was used to being watched. He was the star but never showy. Even under Maggie's female gaze, he signaled a sense of compassion rather than pride, which buoyed her. That smart women will vie for his attention at college actually comforted her: he should not be without adoration. Body and soul, he was a man of beauty.

Beneath her hat and sunglasses, she sighed deeply. Leaning against Gertrude, she drifted to sleep. Even the occasional roar of the enthusiastic crowd didn't stir her. Gertrude smoothed the blanket over their three laps and smiled at Roland. He slipped his arm behind Maggie to support her on the bleacher. They were gleeful to find themselves in this intimate position.

"Our very own Juliette," Gertrude whispered.

Roland winked and smiled.

Gertrude cooked a sweet and savory Indian feast the night of Rip's 18th birthday: chicken tikka, lamb kebabs, chutney, naan and roti, mint sauce, curried potatoes, and much more. Rip's uncle and two cousins attended, as well as Rip's buddies, including a former girlfriend named Melinda, a seriously muscled blonde tennis player. At Gertrude's insistence, Maggie slept over. Rip watched with fascination as she dabbed her fingers in a cup of water in the bathroom mirror, carefully peeling the painted flowers off her face. She stuck them on a sheet of computer paper—a memento for him.

"Your uncle looks like you," Maggie said after washing her face and hands.

"My father and uncle looked like twins," Rip said.

She handed him a small gift, wrapped in cloth and tied with ribbon. It was an early self-portrait in an oval wooden frame she found in a thrift shop. This one was not in the style of Rembrandt but after one of the Flemish Virgin Marys she'd seen in Arthur's book. A robin rested on her shoulder, and she called it "The Annunciation." Rip looked at the bare nail hammered into the wall above his bed and slipped the loop on the back of the painting over it.

"Thank you, Maggie. This nail has been empty for a very long time. Someone gave me a crucifix after my father died," he said. "I found it scary as a little kid. When I was tall enough to reach it standing on the bed, I hid it in my closet. The nail has been waiting for your portrait ever since."

A second gift came in the form of a striptease, complete with exaggerated comic expressions, as she hummed a little tune, twirling each piece of clothing to the floor, tipping her youthful Mediterranean torso with budding hips and breasts this way and that, turning slowly front to back.

"Carol and I were obsessed with the movies of Lili St. Cyr, queen of Burlesque, when we first met," she told Rip as they fell asleep. "I collected negligees and sequined dresses and cut them up and sewed them into risqué costumes." She laughed. "Once, Carol safety-pinned a fake Dalmatian fur around her bare collarbones, like a luxurious leopard skin, but was actually from one of Mick's stuffed animals in the back of his closet. Carol usually preferred bad-ass old gigantic bras she stuffed with cotton, garter belts, seamed stockings, and gold woven belts she tied in various ways. Stevie was privy to some of our early acts and was thoroughly entertained, even if removing our tops was as far as we went."

Tangled in Rip's arms again was humbling. Waking in the darkness, her courage swelled even as she wept with pleasure at her own sense of experience. Her portrait above Rip's bed was proforma as a work of art, but the fact that her dark brown eyes stared across Rip's room day in and day out was *monumental*. She wondered if she would ever experience this heightened contentment again. Rip embraced not only her creative spirit, he appreciated her maturity. Her ability to be two things at once.

The following week, at her request, Stevie let her drive his truck around an empty parking lot before jumping out at the New York State Department of Motor Vehicles in Kingston. The driver's handbook had been simple to memorize and to pass the driver's permit test, she only needed to answer fifteen out of twenty questions in each section correctly. Half of the questions seemed to be about the consequences of driving under the influence of drugs and alcohol rather than the rules and regulations of the road. An hour after dropping her off, Stevie was elated when he spotted her coming out of the building with her thumbs-up. Her success soothed him. Being an only kid to a sick parent was rough. His mother had moved on to a new life in California long ago. A birthday card with a ten-dollar bill was the most he ever received from her.

Meanwhile, the realtor had begun showing the house. As promised, Maggie kept the house picked up—the kitchen table and counters clean, the living room dusted, the beds made, even the windows free of little fingerprints whenever the realtor called to show the house. When there weren't appointments, she cleaned the kitchen cabinets and the hall closet, then started on her room by putting away her face paints. However, scouring the flowers stuck to the wall ruined the paint. She spackled and smoothed the rough spots and, when dry, sanded them down, figuring she'd find leftover wall paint in the garage. It was then that she realized John's December visit was as much about prepping the house to sell as a family visit, which meant that Julia must have known about the move back then. Maggie agreed that it was cost-effective to raise all your kids under one roof. If the move was a shock to Maggie, it was also, as Stevie pointed out, a solution. Julia would have been stuck when Maggie moved to the city. She hoped John and Julia would find happiness, but if not, the twins would have two parents to raise them. In that case, maybe Julia could be the one to get her own apartment down the block. Since Christmas Eve, she and Julia had grown more relaxed with each other. They were natural allies. Perhaps some physical distance would give them much-needed breathing room.

"We are getting a puppy when we move to California," Mia said. "I'm going to call her Jingles!"

"Like Jingle Bells?" Maggie said. She brushed Mia's hair and tried to put the braided headband on, but Mia took it off. "What is she going to look like?"

"Like the picture you made me for Christmas."

"Oh!" Maggie said. "The yellow dog with the floppy ears." Maggie loved holding Mia's silky hair in her hands, so unlike her own. "Mia, would you like to go camping with me, Stevie, and Mick and sleep in a tent and cook over a fire?"

She jumped up and down. "And roast marshmallows!"

Maggie winced as she let Mia's small, happy voice burn a groove in her brain, something she could play over again in her head. Mia will grow up quickly in California without her own loving attention. She wanted to pick a date to visit her family, but everything was up for grabs—money, time, home, relationships, work.

"Come on, guys," Maggie called. "The realtor is coming to show the house!"

The library was Maggie's planned destination, but the day was warm, and feeling low on energy, she steered them toward the playground at the school. Once there, the twins just sat with her on a bench instead of playing, so they headed out on a walking adventure around the backside of the golf course toward the bird sanctuary. The barred owl, the most beautiful wild creature Maggie had ever seen, had been set free. Still, she wanted to show the twins the other birds.

"When I grow up, I'm going to be like the barred owl," Maggie told the twins.

"You are grown up," Mick said.

"And I want to hoot like an owl, too," she continued. She gave it a try, and all three of them hooted together. "And I want to fly like an owl."

After crossing Route 375, Maggie began to run, and the twins followed. Flapping their outstretched arms, they wheeled past the houses at the edge of the golf course. At the dead end, they disappeared down a trail into the woods.

FIFTEEN

STACKS of hardcover copies of *Beach Music* and *The Horse Whisperer*—a truly gruesome story that had sold fifteen million copies—filled the right front window of the bookshop. *Swimming Around the World*, Carol's parents' book, was in the window to the left of the door, along with other books by local authors—Alf Evers' perennial seller, *Woodstock*; Elliott Landy's book *Woodstock: A Spiritual Moment in Time*; and various books on hiking the Catskills and hunting wild edibles. Once a week, Maggie straightened the kid's section. Nostalgic about saying goodbye to the twins, she used her discount to buy a chapter book for them, preferring the classics to the new releases. Her latest find was *My Side of the Mountain*, written in 1959, a fictional story about a boy running away to the Catskills. Maggie crossed her fingers that Julia and John would continue her tradition of reading aloud, as the pleasure thus far had fallen only to Maggie

One small chore Maggie enjoyed was alphabetizing books by the author, particularly the large fiction section. Concentrating on the letters of the authors' names was a way of taking the names out of context. She knew nothing about abstract art, but this little alphabet game made her curious. She added the Whitney and the Museum of Modern Art to her to-do list. The science section of the bookstore also caused her to linger over the shelves. She was fascinated to learn, for instance, in *Swimming Around the World*, that salt separates from fresh water when it freezes, thus enabling wildlife and people to live in the frozen wilderness for years at a time. This fact seemed important to Maggie as she would soon be navigating the world on her own. Scientific facts might help in a scrape. Teresa kept a stack of *The New York Times Book Review* and Tuesday's *Science Times* behind the cashier's desk, which she began to read.

In her third week of shelving books, Teresa called Maggie into her office. "Your work ethic is terrific," she said. "You're early to work, you don't come to work stoned or eat while you work or read while you shelve books, you don't flirt with George, and you're friendly with customers. George is leaving for a summer vacation in June, and I'd like you to take over at the cash register while he's gone. You're turning sixteen, right?"

"Yes," Maggie said. She looked down from the loft where she sat with Teresa. George waved from his perch at the cash register. "What days and hours?" Maggie asked.

"You still pick up the twins at school, right? So let's keep your same hours for now. The beginning pay rate at the cash register is $6.00 an hour, up from $4.25. Just so you know, there is a lot more responsibility."

"I'm aware of that."

"George is very good. He'll train you."

Teresa and Maggie's mom had been friends since the 1970s when the bookstore opened, and it became the hub for women's consciousness-raising meetings. Maggie liked hearing the stories about their protests on the village green, calling for gender equality and equal pay for equal work, including minimum wage for stay-at-home parents. Julia had also worked at the bookstore on and off, but that was before Maggie was born. Teresa relied on part-timers. Since they all trained each other, it was only a bit more paperwork, and she never had to advertise for help. She gave everyone two weeks. If they didn't catch on by then, she let them go. Not many worked the cash register. That was a different kind of position, and Maggie knew her mother had as much to do with her moving up as her work ethic. The next time Carol stopped by the bookstore, she was surprised to find Maggie sitting behind the check-out desk with George.

"I'm looking for a book for Mom's birthday," Carol said, picking up a copy of *The Horse Whisperer* from the stack on the front window. "I'll take this. She doesn't usually like best sellers but reads them as research."

"Would you like it gift-wrapped?" Maggie asked.

"Sure, Maggie, my darling," Carol said. "Don't forget to bring the twins over for cake at seven."

Maggie tore a sheet of shiny white paper from a roll behind her, folded it around the book, and taped the edges. Twisting a polka-dot black and white ribbon over the front and around the back, she knotted it. Her thumb against a single blade of the scissors, she curled the ribbon. "That's $4.95, plus tax. The total is $5.35."

"Bye, sweetie," Carol said, taking her change from a ten-dollar bill. She waved to George and tucked the gift into her backpack. The little bell rang over the door as she exited.

With her own birthday around the corner, time seemed to speed up again. She worried how fast time could go if she wasn't careful, almost as if she really could control the speed of time. Maggie scheduled her driving test, but complications from Lefty's surgery kept Stevie in the city. Rip offered to practice driving with her, but his tennis schedule was crazy. Julia was frazzled with packing and moving arrangements. The bookstore kept Maggie busy, even as most of her belongings were packed in boxes and stacked in Carol's parent's garage, and she still hadn't decided where to live once John's house sold. With the library exhibit opening in two weeks, she mailed and handed out postcards announcing the show. Ms. James had selected Julia's portrait, the one Maggie gave to her at Christmas, for the front of the card, which was included in the show but not for sale. Maggie photocopied the announcement and posted flyers around town as she had for the production of *King Lear in Fourteen Words*. Each evening, Maggie studied the Library show on her desktop as she struggled to write her talk. She wanted it to tell a story that would smack everybody's cheek with a kiss.

May first, Rip and Maggie held hands as they hiked the switchbacks up Overlook. She was grateful for his gentle pull on the steep path. Mountain laurel was budding, goldfinches flitted in the bushes, and she heard the call of the red-eyed vireo, a bird song she knew from the sanctuary. Finally, she spotted one on a branch right in front of her.

At the ranger's cabin, she led Rip down a small path to a stone overhang that dropped a full, dizzying thirteen hundred feet. Careful not to go near the edge, they scanned the names and dates carved into the ledge: J. Papa Nicholas, 1889; Dwight Jenkins, 1973; C.S.T., 1913.

"Smokin' Jerry was here, 1856-1913," Maggie read aloud. "It sounds like he might have fallen."

"Or jumped," said Rip.

"I can't imagine people carving their names into the stone ledge with chisels, inches from death."

"My grandfather kept a diary when he was my age—about the depression, losing all but the stone house in Rhinebeck, and his enchantment of Thomas Cole's religious visions of the Catskills."

"There is a mountain named after Cole," Maggie said. "I read that he slept in a wigwam of deciduous branches on Overlook and saw the stars below!" Her eyes widened. "And I read that early sailors coming up the Hudson blamed Eve for mountains like they were monsters. Cole's beautiful paintings of the Catskills put an end to that superstition."

The clear view at the top was transcendent, but as they began to climb the metal fire lookout, it vibrated in the wind, and they decided to skip it. Maggie unpacked a baguette, a hunk of cheese, two apples, and a bar of chocolate. She glanced around for the stranger, but he was nowhere to be seen. Rip noticed her look of concern.

"What time is it?" she asked.

"You have exactly five minutes before you turn sixteen. Did I tell you my mother calls you Juliette?"

Maggie laughed and reached across the picnic table for his hand. "Then you are my Romeo. Shakespeare has written our story."

"No, we're rewriting it," he insisted.

Rip was beginning to know Maggie, how to say something sweet or savory to take her mind away from troubling thoughts. And minutes later, on the hour, she saw the man she was looking for, camouflaged against the brown rock at the shady edge of the woods. He was familiar, after all, no longer a stranger. She pulled a postcard from her backpack and broke off a piece of chocolate. Walking toward him, he stood.

"Happy birthday," he said.

Maggie gasped. "How did you know?"

"I've watched you many years eating birthday cake with your mother on this day."

Her head swarmed with bees. She could hardly speak. "Julia is selling the house. I'm moving to the city in the fall...I may not see you next year."

"I will always climb the mountain on May first."

She gave him the piece of chocolate and held out the postcard announcing her library exhibit. He gazed knowingly at the image of Julia. Maggie moved closer to look at the postcard together. "Please come to my opening," she said. Turning, she skipped back to Rip.

SIXTEEN

THE FORGET-ME-NOTS PAINTED across Maggie's nose and cheeks matched her China-blue headdress. She wore large fake pearl earrings, a white collar, and a simple gold lamé dress. Arriving early for her opening reception at the library, she caught her reflection in the window and stared into her own brown eyes. Then she circled through the various rooms of the library—art, fiction, children's literature, history. She paused before each of her simple paintings, bidding them a final goodbye. She loved them all, even as a naive attempt to capture Woodstock in an old-world style. Signs posted in each room read: *Paintings by Maggie Pierce are fifty dollars each. Fifty percent of sales will go toward the library's spring fundraiser.* As neighbors and friends arrived, Maggie took a seat in a straight-back wooden chair between bookshelves and focused on the note cards on her lap.

In the last weeks before the show, Maggie painted a handful of new portraits from drawings in her sketchbook to switch up the exhibition. There was one of Julia wearing her health food store apron, a portrait of Lucy, the twins' teacher, and a portrait of a woman who protested on the village green on Sundays with a group of other white-haired women who lovingly called themselves *the hags*.

The main room of the library quickly filled, and with a nod from Ms. James, Maggie stood. She saw Gertrude, Roland, Rip, Stevie and Fern, Lucy, Beth and Pilar, Arthur and Kate, even the artist Nell from the Woodstock School of Art, and a couple of Gertrude's friends from her opening. A cluster of local high school students mumbled and shuffled in the doorway.

"Hello, everyone. I am Anna Magdalena Pierce, better known as Maggie or Flowers to some." She smiled at Rip. "My mother, Julia, named me after Johann Sabastian Bach's second wife, a woman uncompromisingly devoted to art. I was born sixteen years ago at Old Red, a communal house at the confluence of Beaverkill Creek and the Cascade Brook. Kate, Arthur, Lefty, two-year-old Stevie, and several others were in attendance. Julia's labor included a lot of hours, but those at Old Red agreed that mine was a textbook birth. Arthur put a pencil in my hand at age four and taught me to draw without looking at the page. Later, my favorite pastime was a game called Exquisite Corpse, with adults and children drawing together in turns. The first person folds a piece of paper many times, draws on one section, folds it so no one can see it, and then passes it to the second person, who uses one line from the previous drawing to begin their own image. This game has been ongoing at Old Red for twenty-six years. Flipping through its many humorous drawings entertained me growing up. At around age seven, Arthur—can you raise your hand, please?"

Like a bird peeking out of the leafy woods, the lip of Arthur's worn red baseball cap tilted into the air, his gray fuzzy hair springing out in plumes.

"Thank you. Arthur began taking me with him to sketch birds and trees. He studied art at Yale and taught me to carefully turn the pages of his beloved art books. He set up a space for me in a corner of his studio with an easel and paints. When I was twelve, a mirror appeared, and I painted my first self-portraits." Maggie pointed to a far corner where the group of them hung. "I dressed up like a Rembrandt with pillows beneath a bedspread pinned at my neck. Posing is something I like to do." Maggie turned sideways and gazed over her shoulder at the audience, her rosy lips parted as she had practiced in the reflection of the window. "Can anyone guess which artist I am paying homage to today?"

Someone yelled: "Vermeer. *The Girl with the Pearl Earring*."

"Yes. Thanks go to Pilar for loaning me this gorgeous dress from her theater closet. Where are you, Pilar?"

She raised her hand, and Maggie continued. "So, these thirty-one paintings are of us, our Woodstock community. If you'd like to play NAME THAT MODEL, Ms. James has a sheet for you to fill out. The first person to correctly name each of my subjects wins a small portrait like these, which I will paint for you. And don't forget, this is a library fundraiser. Fifty percent of all sales go toward the library."

The crowd stirred, and Maggie took a deep breath. "I'd like to thank Ms. James for curating this show and her whole library staff for their encouragement and kindness." Maggie blew a kiss to the audience. "I love you all."

As Ms. James stepped up to the microphone to make her announcements, a woman clasped Maggie's hand, pulling her aside. With hair like straw, watery green eyes, and wrinkled tan skin, she searched Maggie's face. "Do you know me?" she asked. "You were only four years old when I left Woodstock. I caught you as Julia pushed you through the birth canal. Six pounds, four ounces. Lots of dark hair. Your dark, sleepy eyes opened. You are as beautiful today as the day you were born."

"Agnus?"

She nodded. Her face cracked into a laugh. Tears filled her eyes.

Maggie threw her arms around Agnus and whispered in her ear: "I'm so happy to see you. I'm doing my best for Stevie, but I am an imperfect sister. Lefty and Stevie miss you so badly."

"I'm here to stay, Maggie. Julia wrote to me about Lefty's leg and now cancer… and she's worried about leaving you behind. So I'm here for you, too."

Agnus receded into the crowded library as others frolicked to Maggie's side or squeezed toward Ms. James to receive paper and pencil to play Name That Model. Town folk gazed at each other in the small library and whispered to each other in front of the miniature paintings until the place was buzzing. Others spilled onto the grass, where Julia set a table of fruit and cookies, iced tea, and lemonade. Maggie spotted Stevie and Fern on the rope swing hanging from the old oak tree growing on the huge lawn and ran to them.

"Your mother is back, Stevie!" Maggie said, hugging him. "Amazing!"

"I know. She wanted to surprise you," Stevie said. "She drove in last night."

Gertrude, followed by Roland and a small Asian man in a straw hat, stepped through the library door. They paused at the refreshment table, where Julia poured them cups of lemonade. She introduced herself and walked with them toward Maggie.

"Congratulations, Maggie," Gertrude said. "Wonderful show, and I'm delighted to meet your mother." She reached out for Julia's arm. Roland and his friend circled around the swing where Maggie stood. A gust of wind blew hair, skirts, and scarves into the blue sky as the man in the gray suit held onto his hat. Gertrude continued. "I'd like you to meet a friend, Charlie Kim, a collector from the city."

"Congratulations," said Charlie, touching his hat. He offered

Maggie his card. "Your paintings are intriguing. Even the signature—like Whistler's—a flower and the date." He opened a photocopied handout of the show to a portrait of Arthur, dated 1991. "You painted this at age eleven?"

"Yes. Arthur was painting a tree, and I painted him."

Rip's fingers tickled Maggie's hand as he stood behind her. "Well done, Maggie Pierce," he whispered. Their equally dark eyes flashed at each other for a complex moment. Her paintings harkened to a younger self, yet, surrounded by new acquaintances, she felt accomplished. Her whole body rippled and shimmered like she felt standing at the precipice of Overlook. His white shirt was rolled to his elbow, and she quietly cupped his solid forearm with both hands.

"Meet at the Millstream!" Fern called as she and Stevie slipped out of the crowd toward Tinker Street.

"Give me a call when you are in the city next," said Charlie Kim. "Bring some of your sketches. I'd like to see more of your work."

"I will. Thank you," she said. Looking again at his crisp card, she noted his address on East 72nd Street.

Rip bent to her ear. "The stranger from Overlook stands in the window."

Julia's eyes steered into Maggie like headlights. Agnus fearfully clutched Julia. Rip tugged Maggie out from behind the group that had gathered around her and focused on the small window panes of the library. The stranger's image skewed as he vanished.

The tension faded as Julia greeted Rip, and Maggie introduced him to Agnus. Then Rip and Maggie made a break. Strolling across the lawn, she spilled her confusion. "Have you ever dreamed of something so complex, like a movie that seems to go on for years? And the dream literally wears you out. You want so badly to wake up that the end comes fast, and you're scrambling to understand what's happening. Suddenly, everything is so unnaturally sewn up. The mystery is gone, and you open your eyes, disappointed. The dream vanishes completely. And you think nothing else of any importance will ever happen."

"Is the monk your father?" Rip whispered.

"Is he a monk?"

"Yes, don't you think?"

Her face turned sunny. "So that's why Stevie has been after me to study zazen."

SEVENTEEN

AGNUS WAS present at John's house for the last supper. Maggie made a mushroom lemon risotto, steamed red snapper, and a green salad. Aside from a squabble between the twins, it was a quiet night on the Millstream. Stevie and Fern were attending one of their many pre-graduation parties, and everyone turned in early. Agnus slept in Stevie's spot on the living room couch. Twelve hours later, the packed moving van pulled out of the driveway to begin its three-thousand-mile trek to California, and the goodbyes were upon them. As the twins climbed into the back seat of Agnus' station wagon, Maggie noticed that only one bluebird feather remained on Mick's Sizzling Strings hat.

"Maggie, sit next to me!" Mia called.

"I'm not going with you, Mia. Remember?" She gave Mia a kiss. "I'll visit once you settle in California. Send me some drawings of your new house."

Julia unrolled the passenger window for a last hug. "I'm proud of you, Maggie. Take care of yourself. I left John's number on the kitchen counter. Call me."

"I love you, Ma."

Maggie's words made Julia unexpectedly tear up. There was joy in letting go. She had raised Maggie. Living at Old Red had been a success. Now, she crossed her fingers that California would be a good move for the twins.

"I'll be back in a few days," Agnus called to Maggie from the driver's seat. "I'm dropping them at the airport and then checking in at the midtown Marriott. Stevie's coming into town tomorrow night, so we'll visit Lefty together."

The Millstream echoed inside John's house, empty except for her mother's baby grand piano. Maggie sat at the piano and then got up to open the bench. Her mother's music in hand-written tablature was where it had always been, along with her mother's favorite pieces by Anna Magdalena Bach. Julia had taught Maggie beginning lessons, but she didn't practice. Piano was her mother's love. Now, for the first time, she wished she could really play. Now that the baby grand was scheduled to be moved back to Kate and Arthur's at Big Red. Now that her mother wouldn't be there to fill the room with music.

When she closed the lid, she stepped out onto the screened porch. The day was already muggy. She didn't expect Stevie until five when his shift at the hardware store ended. With the whole day ahead of her, she changed from her pajamas into her bikini, grabbed the book Carol loaned her, and laid on her favorite rock in the middle of the stream. Staring up down the stream, she committed the moment to memory. With two nights left at the house, she planned to eat the leftovers in the fridge and whatever else she could find in the cupboard. In three days, she had to deliver John's house broom clean, and then she'd move to Carol's.

After Agnus' car passed by Carol's with Julia and the kids, Carol ate a bowl of cereal and slipped through the neighbor's side garden along the well-worn path to Maggie's. She shivered at the emptiness upon opening the front door. The couch where she and Stevie smooched so many nights was gone. The table where they ate lunch with the twins no longer existed. Carol would be the first to admit that she needed a full refrigerator, ample allowance, and family vacations. She raised money for charity, but she had not yet held a job. Maggie was an anomaly. Carol knew of no one at her private school or Woodstock as independent. Spotting Maggie streamside, she picked her way to its edge like a deer.

"How are you?"

Maggie nodded. "Okay. This book is amazing. We should find these ancient plays and perform them in Central Park one day."

"I like that idea," Carol said.

"And start a green thumb garden devoted to family planning. Really! Did you read it? Listen to this: Greeks, Romans, and Egyptians used the juice of giant fennel called silphium, which contained the chemical ferula, to terminate pregnancy. Pennyroyal contains a chemical called pulegone, which also terminates pregnancy. The seeds of Queen Anne's Lace block the hormone progesterone. Rue and pomegranate seeds prevent pregnancy and induce abortion. Another method to prevent pregnancy was plant fiber mixed with acacia gum and honey together to cover the cervix."

"Mom worries about me," Carol said.

"Why?"

"Guilt. Shame. Anger. They drain the ego. That's what she felt when she had an abortion at my age. Hers was illegal. Women and doctors back then were thrown in jail. It was a witch hunt."

Maggie closed the book. "Was your mother unable to get pregnant after her abortion?"

"She chose to adopt rather than ever become pregnant again." Carol laid back on the towel. "Did you catch the part toward the end of the book where it cites evidence that after Medieval times, women's information about family planning could only be passed in secret? The laws of politics, religion, and medicine ruled over women's bodies. And women couldn't read."

"And the institution of marriage," Carol added.

Maggie closed the book. "What's the best type of birth control?"

"Pills. I have an IUD. It's okay. For some women, it's painful. A diaphragm is another choice. It's a matter of finding what works best for you. But always use a condom."

Maggie laughed. "You sound like Lefty."

Carol joined in, laughing. "Condom is one of his favorite words."

The next day, Maggie arrived at the bookstore an hour before opening. Once in, she locked the door again and began the housekeeping chores—transferring cash from the safe to the till, the weekly dusting, and vacuuming. The ancient rubber plant on the counter tended to drop its small soft leaves over the weekend when tourists crowded the store. Sometimes, friends slipped notes to her through the transom, as it was difficult to get ahold of her since John's phone was disconnected. Miriam stopped by once a week to check in with her. Kids from high school dropped in to let her know about a party. Arthur left a paper bag of things he found around the house, including a partially used sketchbook and her bat mitzvah notebook.

At noon, she unlocked the door and greeted shoppers. She always looked up when the bell rang, but when no one was around, she sketched people licking cream cones on the sidewalk, the old hippies smoking and strumming guitars on the green, and tourists who paused in front of the store windows to read book covers. Fern came by to say hi and said that Lefty's goats had been sold. Lefty was already blowing in the wind.

Maggie's eyes teared. She decided to buy a mobile phone next time she was in the city.

"I'm okay," Maggie told Gertrude when she took her out for a sandwich at the bakery on Tinker Street. "I have three fathers and two mothers. Arthur, you met at the opening. Lefty, Stevie's dad, who is recovering from lung cancer, and my sperm donor, although I don't know him. Plus Julia and Agnus. You met Stevie's mom, Agnus. She was a midwife back then. She delivered me."

Gertrude nodded and sipped her cup of hot black coffee. "I received good news yesterday about a grant, and I'd like to hire you to work with me for two months. It's a research position. I'm writing a book."

"Oh, exciting! But you must know lots of brilliant college students."

"I do hire lots of students, but this project involves a knowledge of art and an open perspective on society. You are visual and verbal and have a rare sense of independence, a must for all creative thinkers. Rip told me you got your driver's license, which is perfect timing. We have an extra car you can use. You can stay in my studio behind the house—it has a fold-out bed and a bathroom. And feel free to use the kitchen in the house."

"What's the book?"

"It's about icons."

"Do you mean the little icons on my computer or the religious kind?"

"Excellent question. I'm interested in icons, in general, as the intersection of verbal and visual communication. Their power, purpose, use, and misuse. The cultural conditions that allow the development of icons. And how a person becomes one."

"As in?"

Gertrude smiled. "Who comes to mind?"

"Marilyn Monroe," Maggie said. "How much does the research position pay?"

"Four thousand dollars for eight weeks, full-time. But remember, you've got to pay taxes out of that. And the work needs to be done at the Bard College library. Without the internet, I would never attempt this kind of project. A computer science student will teach you the programs and best research sites."

Maggie grinned. "I'm all yours as soon as I figure it out with Teresa at the bookstore."

"I have some traveling to do this summer, so I won't be around much. Roland usually comes with me if it's Europe. We'll probably spend a week in Morocco with friends as well. Rip has his five-week tennis clinic in England. Does it sound too lonely?"

"Not a problem."

Gertrude clapped her hands. "Brava!"

Maggie tucked the uneaten half of her sandwich into her bag, and they walked together to Gertrude's car, parked in the lot behind the bookstore. It was the copper-colored Honda that Maggie and Stevie saw in her Rhinebeck driveway. She wondered if this was the car she would drive. Gertrude's plan meant cutting short her summer with Carol, but no matter. By fall, they'd both be living in the city. She'd have close to six thousand dollars saved—one thousand from her bat mitzvah and one thousand from babysitting and odd jobs. And now Gertrude's.

Maggie waited as the Honda was backed out of the lot. It was daunting to think of driving a car every day, but Maggie knew she'd get used to it. She knew her way around all the back roads. As she waved goodbye, Gertrude pulled up close and unrolled the window. "I forgot to mention, feel free to make some art in my studio, too. Call me when you get a start date."

"Thank you," Maggie said. "Really. For everything."

Maggie watched the Honda turn onto Tinker Street but remained rooted to the gravel parking lot. Stumped by Gertrude's generous offer, every cell in her body snapped. Her senses rang like bells. Fearless joy. This must be what Petit felt on his tightrope. It's the feeling you get when you accept the chance of falling, and knowing you won't let it happen.

EIGHTEEN

AFTER SWEEPING debris into the center of each room of John's house, Maggie scooped what she could into garbage bags and set them out by the driveway for Stevie's dump run. Then she carried yet another box of her belongings to Carol's house and made some phone calls. Rip didn't pick up, but she left a message inviting him to camp out with her in the empty house. Maggie was sensitive about keeping the line free for Carol's parents, who worked from home, so she postponed a call to Julia. Instead, she made one last quick one to Ms. James.

"Hold on," said the librarian at the main desk. "Thank you for holding," said the librarian. "Ms. James is in a meeting. She asked if you could stop by sometime this week."

Maggie peeked out the bedroom door at Joan, sitting erect in front of her computer at the dining room table, which was covered in organized piles of paper. She was so grateful Carol's family had taken her in, yet now she was suddenly leaving. She needed to alert them to her change of plans. Maggie cleared her throat as she walked toward her.

"Hi, Maggie," Joan said without looking up.

"Good morning, Joan. Did you see I made applesauce? No sugar, only cinnamon."

"Delicious. I had some for breakfast."

"If you guys are around, I'd like to make dinner Saturday night since Carol won't be back from Poughkeepsie until late Friday. Maybe some homemade pasta with pesto and a big salad."

"Sure. We have an extra ticket for the graduation ceremony Thursday afternoon if you'd like to join us."

"Thanks, but the piano mover is coming, and I'm working at the bookstore. I turn in the keys on Saturday, so I've got to finish at Ma's."

"I wish we could offer you your own room."

"I'm fine. It feels like home."

"So, who are our new neighbors?"

"A family with two young kids. I don't know if they'll be weekenders or move to Woodstock full-time."

Town was still quiet on weekdays in June. Lilac, peonies, iris, wisteria, and purple allium bloomed on the green. Maggie propped open the bookstore door to take in the sweet air, leaving the screen door closed. Miriam, one of the counselors from the high school, was the first customer of the day.

"Hello, Miriam!" Maggie smiled.

"Hey, look who's running the store!" Miriam said with a big smile. "I thought you were shelving books, and now I see you're behind the cash register." She put her purse down on the counter and pulled out an envelope. "I downloaded an application for you, Maggie. Take a look at it and let me know if you are interested in applying. I think it's exactly what you said you were looking for. It's a two-year fellowship with a dance company in the West Village starting in October. It comes with a stipend plus room and board. But I think it's going to be competitive. You're going to have to work hard on the application."

"But I'm not a dancer," Maggie said.

"That doesn't matter. The work is more like assisting the director. Like what you did in monitoring class at the Woodstock School of Art. Like taking charge of Mick and Mia to help your mother. Some cleaning and cooking and some administrative work. The biggest problem is your age. But with excellent recommendations, I think an exception might be made. You've got Beth from the bird sanctuary and the fiber artist; what's her name?"

"Pilar."

"That's right," Miriam continued. "And Nell at the Woodstock School of Art; Ms. James. And Teresa. I'll write a recommendation explaining your family situation and the responsibility you took on helping your mother with the twins."

"Thanks," Maggie said. Fern's comment on not wanting to leave the magic of Woodstock hit her hard. New York City was going to be a far different experience. She wouldn't have all her mother's friends helping her out. "You're amazing, Miriam."

"Oh, please. There are plenty of fuck-ups in this town," she laughed. "I try to help young people who help themselves. You've earned this, Maggie. Write the first draft, and I'll go over it with you. The deadline is August 15th, so you have some time. But let's get it in early."

All was quiet during the last hour of her shift until a noisy convertible sports car pulled up across the green, and Maggie looked up. A man stepped out of it wearing a British-looking hat with a brim.

Maggie smiled when she saw who it was. "Can I help you?"

"Yes," he said, leaning in.

She placed her hands on Rip's smooth cheeks and her lips on his. Her boss, Teresa, was clicking away at her computer in the mezzanine. The only customers were two middle school boys in the back reading graphic novels.

"Are you ready to go?" he asked.

"In ten minutes. What are you driving?"

"My father's TR6. A Triumph. I do my best to keep it running."

Maggie's eyes widened. "It's a beautiful day. Let's drive out to the Ashokan Reservoir to see the bald eagles."

With Maggie in the driver's seat, feeling her way through the gears, she headed up Tinker Street. Shifting into fourth on the Bearsville flats, then down to third at the Y in Bearsville, she again shifted on the curves of Shady. At the top of Lake Hill, she sailed across the Willow flats and on down alongside the Beaverkill. She pulled over in front of Old Red.

"This is where I lived until age twelve. See the second-floor window above the living room? That was originally Julia's room. That's where I was born. And when the twins were born, it became a nursery."

"How many kids?"

"Eventually, seven. It was set up like a dorm with single beds." She pointed across the road. "We swam under that bridge in Ideal Park, an 1880s utopian community. I saw photographs. The main building was the kitchen and dining room. Another was a bathhouse. Surrounding those were seven or eight sleeping cabins. Of course, now they are all rebuilt as single-family homes."

Revving the engine, she pulled back out onto Route 212. "John Chapman, aka Johnny Appleseed, passed through here, planting apple trees along the way. There's a plaque for him back in Bearsville. Greening apples. They make great pies."

From the Ashokan promenade, a view of Slide Mountain reflected in the eleven-mile span of water, its steep rustic trails hidden in deciduous trees. Halfway across the promenade, Rip spotted a young eagle as it flew down from a tall stand of evergreens. Several other young eagles followed, diving for trout, bass, or perch, not bothered by the dozen or so humans below.

"Stevie and I raced on rollerblades here."

"You won?"

"He won half the time."

"You are going to make a good wife, Maggie."

"Who's marrying?"

"Maybe one day?"

She shrugged.

After Chinese take-out, Rip blew up a mattress, and they nested in sleeping bags on the screened porch back at John's. He clicked a flashlight on a photograph and passed it to her. It was of Maggie and the stranger on Overlook.

"What?" She took the flashlight from him to study it. Side by side, the two looked directly into the camera. She remembered the moment but wasn't aware that Rip took a photograph. Both noses had the signature tear-drop nostrils.

"What do you say?" Rip said.

"Thank you so much," she said. "I can show this to Stevie now and pose my question. Isn't that what siblings are for? To figure out the parents? By the way, Rip, how are you feeling about Gertrude's plan to hire me for the summer? And living with me? Are you up for it? I know you'll be in England most of the time..."

Rip was up on his elbow, and now he laid back, wrapping his arm around her shoulder. She snuggled against him, their legs and feet entwined. "I canceled my tournament," he said. "I never intended to be a tennis star. Until meeting you, I was just going along with my coach. Besides, I saw how it put you to sleep."

"Don't change your career because of me, Rip."

"I've decided on architecture. It's what my mother wanted to do. My father loved architecture. It's Roland's passion. He spoke to a colleague about an internship in the city, and we met. It sounds interesting. So I'll take the train every morning. The days will be long, but we can spend the nights together."

She shut her eyes, listening to the music of the Millstream as she always had. Her head rippled with mountain water, tapping the boulders like keys. "I'll drop you off at the station on my way to Bard in the morning; I'll pick you up in the evening. We'll make dinner together, watch a movie, and fall asleep after sex. Isn't that what married people do?" Feeling the pressure of their short eight weeks together, she said: "We'll be first partners."

He shook his head. "Let's mate like eagles."

"For real?"

NINETEEN

THE LIBRARY on Tinker Street was back to its familiar quiet old book smell when Maggie stopped by to see Ms. James, but she wasn't in. Maggie didn't know the nearly bald man with a long string of braid down his back. He gave her an envelope with her name scrawled in blue ink.

"Thank you," Maggie said. "I'd like to pick up the paintings, too. Did she leave a bag of them for me?"

The frail man braced his hands on the desk and slowly lifted into a standing position. After searching the area behind the checkout desk, he flapped his hand against his loose pants. "I don't see any paintings."

"They're small pieces of wood," she said. When he drew a blank, she continued. "Okay, thanks for looking. I'll call Ms. James."

Inhaling the green summer air, Maggie sat on the swing on the library lawn and opened the envelope:

Congratulations, Maggie. Your show sold out. Twelve people bought paintings—see the list enclosed—and someone named Charles Kim bought the remaining eighteen! Your mother's portrait is safe in my office for you to pick up. I wish you luck in your move to New York City. Please stay in touch. Ms. James.

P.S. The winner of the contest is Pilar Torres. See her contact info below.

"Wow," Maggie said aloud. It didn't make sense that Pilar knew Arthur, Kate, Lefty, Carol, and everyone else. *How mysterious,* she thought. Sitting on the swing, she pumped so high her bottom lifted off the seat, and the chain became slack mid-air, nose to nose with Overlook Mountain. Gripping the chain tight as the swing stalled, gravity finally pulled her back to the ground. Dragging her feet, she came to a stop. She figured she'd have seven thousand dollars in the bank by the end of the summer. For the first time, she felt almost self-sufficient. Her confidence soared. On her way back to Carol's house, she dropped the house key off at the realtor's office and stopped by the bank to deposit the library check and the last five hundred Julia owed her.

Carol woke Maggie late Friday night when she arrived back in Woodstock. They lay awake for hours, chatting. Carol told her about the parties, her graduation ceremony, the gossip, and even the break-up with her new literary girlfriend. Maggie was surprised that Carol wasn't the least upset about it. But Saturday night, when Maggie served her apple pie and announced to Carol and her parents her intention to accept Gertrude's research position, Carol slumped in her chair.

"I don't believe this, Maggie," Carol cried. "You've fubbed off living with us to move in with Rip?"

"I didn't fub off," Maggie said. "It's a financial opportunity, and the research interests me. I'll have a car. I promise I'll visit you every week. And in two months, we'll both be living in the city."

"My concern," Joan said hesitantly. "Is… I find it odd that Rip's mother seems to have orchestrated a love nest."

"Don't be surprised if you change your mind about Rip after sleeping with him for a week," Carol added.

Carol's father, Arnie, stepped in and spoke directly to Maggie: "From an early age you've taken on roles beyond your years. Without God or a father to lean on, you have always chosen the road not taken. And you've been an excellent friend to Carol. I stand by you, Maggie. I told Julia as much before she left. I congratulated her for raising a rebel—a revolutionary—in the best sense of the word."

It wasn't until Sunday that Maggie called Julia to inform her of the change in plans. Bolstered by Arnie's support, she wondered what her mother would say.

"Hi, Ma. I'm at Carol's house. Everything is taken care of at John's. The house is broom-clean and locked. I turned the key over to the realtor. And deposited your check."

"Thank you, Maggie. That was a big job."

"I'm working on an application for a two-year fellowship assisting a modern dance company in the West Village. Miriam found it for me. Also, another opportunity turned up. On Monday, I'm starting an eight-week research project at Bard. I'm moving into Gertrude's studio in Rhinebeck. It comes with room and board and a four thousand dollar stipend. She's loaning me a car so I can get around. I'm in good shape, Ma. Did you meet the collector Charlie Kim at the library opening? He bought eighteen paintings. The show sold out. Can you believe it?"

"Yes, I can," Julia said. Her words were unusually slow and drawn. She sounded tired.

"How are you and the twins?" Maggie asked.

"Settling," she said. "Seven-year-old Toby is obliging thus far. We'll see how it goes with Mick and Mia. I think John is happy to have us."

"Are you happy, Ma?"

"Marin County is beautiful. I walk the beach every morning. What's not to love?" Then Julia fell silent. Maggie waited for her mother to continue. Finally, she said: "Have you talked to Stevie or Agnus? Lefty took a turn for the worse, and he's back in the hospital."

"Yikes," Maggie said. "I'll take the bus to the city and visit him. I've decided to buy a phone so I can stay in touch with you and everybody else."

"I'm glad," she said. "Call me when you get it."

Falling in love was not a problem, as Maggie saw it. She wasn't being taken advantage of. Rip was solid, lovingly conceived, and polished like a work of art. He was tender, even lyrical. The night they slept together on the screened porch, he woke singing a sexy little song:

<blockquote>
I build you a house.
I build for you a table.
I hang the flower pot for you
And put cream cheese on your bagel.
</blockquote>

Maggie's confidence in Rip and, likewise Gertrude exceeded her imagination. Gertrude outlined in an email the format for the research: Maggie would be sent one research question each week, meaning that she would have Friday deadlines to submit her findings. The following Monday, a new question based on her previous week's research would appear in her email. There was no wrong answer, Gertrude explained. All information was to be based on her research and express her point of view. Maggie thought it over. The only similar challenge she had attempted was her bat mitzvah preparation. And the most difficult part of that was relating her Torah portion to a personal story and sharing it on the bemah. Maggie was relieved that working with Gertrude would not culminate in a speech. And she wouldn't have to buck Julia, who had not supported her decision to have a bat mitzvah in the first place. It was partially because of the cost of the lessons and the expectation of a party but more because Julia felt Maggie was wasting her time taking on a patriarchal coming-of-age tradition. Maggie's twelve-year-old secret desire was that her father would show up in the congregation and introduce himself.

"I'm curious, Ma," Maggie argued. "You and your mother, my grandmother, are Jewish. And the Jewish religion follows the matriarchal bloodline. So wouldn't you be curious if you were me?"

In the end, Julia called Rabbi Leon, a musician she had performed with at festivals and holidays. He was delighted by Maggie's gumption and put Maggie in touch with a young scholar named Helen. When Helen learned that Maggie would be paying for the tutoring from her own savings, she waived the fee. Week by week, Helen morphed into a fascinating angel in Maggie's eyes. Her attention to detail to the Hebrew pronunciation, inflection, and deep meanings of words and where they came from was like a professional acting lesson. Helen's conservative looks also piqued Maggie's curiosity. She appeared at their house every Monday from four to five with air-brushed hair and make-up, wearing a dress with a slip and the diamond engagement ring on her finger. Maggie did her best to take in Helen's every word, but she had to leave the door ajar to keep her eye on the twins. A videotape didn't guarantee that the twins would stay put. Once, she glanced out the window while making dinner and saw the two of them alone at the edge of the Millstream.

Thinking about her bat mitzvah, Maggie went through boxes in Carol's garage to retrieve the notebook Arthur had dropped off. Flipping through the pages, she was struck by Helen's positivity, her patience, and her prodding. *Learn in bite-sizes,* Helen wrote. *See if you can memorize the blessing that we reviewed. Whenever you practice, jot down in the notebook the date, the time you start, and the time you end. Really work on this prayer so it's totally smooth. Check yourself against the tape. Write down your questions. Keep up the good work! Gorgeous! Very good! Perfect reading! Great Start!*

It felt to Maggie that Helen was peeling back the baby blankets covering Maggie's twelve-year-old brain. Like Arnie, Helen expected Maggie to do the impossible—read and sing in Hebrew. And Helen pushed her to get underneath the story of her Torah portion: *How did it feel reading it? Why? What resonated for you? What part of the story do you want to create a lesson from? Sing the prayers along with the tape. Sing when you're walking into town. Sing the melody before you sleep.*

As Maggie packed for her eight-week move to Rhinebeck, she wondered why some women she loved took a stance against her chosen path while Helen, Ms. James, Miriam, and Gertrude not only embraced her adventuresome spirit but opened doors.

TWENTY

RHINEBECK'S quiet streets were new to Maggie. Its well-kept homes with wide lawns and two or three large old trees were void of people and silent except for an occasional barking dog. Most twilights, after a take-out dinner or one of Maggie's vegetarian dishes and a glass of wine from Roland's cellar, she and Rip walked the family dog, Bernie, toward the edge of town. As the days passed, Maggie noticed shadows of homeowners in the yellow light of windows or the flicker of blue TV screens. Cars backed out of driveways in the morning and returned in the evening. During the whole first week in Rhinebeck, Maggie worked in the studio writing and revising the fellowship application. She made an appointment to pick up the last remaining letter of recommendation from Nell at the Woodstock School of Art. Miriam, who thought of every angle, suggested that when the application was complete, she should hand deliver it. She said it would be an opportunity to make a good impression.

Gertrude's north-facing studio looked out on a tall hedge and stone wall, providing not only ample privacy from neighbors but a private garden with six mature blueberry bushes, a row of dwarf apple trees, and herbs. Maggie came to think of Roland's simple, elegant studio design of concrete and glass as heavenly. Its large bathroom had an open shower and an unusually wide shallow sink. Storage for Gertrude's paintings and drawings was organized on racks above the bathroom, reachable by ladder.

Maggie's first assignment was to create a list of ten personal icons. While she welcomed the challenge and got excited by the goose chase, it felt a bit like Alice's rabbit hole. Her notebook and computer file filled with doodles and words, and she kept plugging along.

One evening, Rip and Maggie walked Bernie down a country road above the Hudson River, hoping to catch a breeze to cut through the humid August air. Rip was riffing on cost analysis, materials, and designs he was working on at his architectural firm internship. Maggie listened with hands clasped behind her back, and, at one point, she brought them forward. At the center of her right palm was a perfectly round dark red circle of what looked like blood.

Maggie showed Rip her hand. "What is it?"

"It looks like blood," he said. "Are you hurt?"

"I'm not. Yikes! Where did it come from? A bird or a tree? Is there more?" She turned around and neither her cutoffs nor shirt nor shoes nor hair had any red dots.

"Oh," he said. "You also have a smaller dot on your forehead."

"Let me check you," she said.

Without discovering any more blood, they turned around and walked back the way they'd come. They searched the sky, the trees, and bushes along the old asphalt road but came up with nothing. Not a speck of red anywhere on the road, in the grass, or ditch. No dead frogs or birds. No car or plane had passed in the last twenty minutes. Rip pried open old Bernie's mouth and searched her four paws to no avail.

"And I don't have my period," Maggie burst out with frustration. She suddenly got creeped out and wiped her hand in a trickle of ditch water.

"It's the stigmata," Rip said, wiping her forehead with a leaf. "The wounds of Jesus. I declare you Saint Anna Magdalena."

"I want a scientific explanation."

"Does it hurt?"

"No wound. My skin is clear."

They returned home and groomed the dog, hoping to find some explanation. They both showered until they felt confident that all blood was washed clean. Wrapped in a towel, Maggie looked up the definition of the word stigmata. It was related to the word stigma, something negative like shame, disgrace, or dishonor. However, the Christian religion changed the definition to mean a mark of divine favor. This only frustrated her. Before falling asleep, Maggie whispered to Rip: "I didn't will it to happen. I'm not religious. Do you believe me?"

"Of course."

"I'm not a witch."

"It's one of the mysteries of the universe. It's something awesome. Not to worry."

"But if you hadn't been there, you might think I'm crazy."

"It's a crazy story."

The next morning, Maggie skipped work. She took the train with Rip into the city to drop off her completed application. Watching the Hudson's beautiful meandering as it widened and narrowed soothed her. At Penn Station, Rip grabbed a cab over to Astor Place while she took the A train to 14th Street and walked south to Bethune. Westbeth was a formidable white stone building. Inside, the ground floor was a giant courtyard with a metal and glass-covered roof at least ten stories high. A long stairway ran up along the inside. Hiking to the third floor, Maggie easily found the Ginger MaGee Dance Studio. A strangely familiar music wafted beneath the door. After a loud knock, a smiling woman, standing only to Maggie's shoulder, motioned for her to enter.

"Welcome," Ginger said. Her hair, the color of her name, swooped into a bob tied with a turquoise scarf on top of her head.

She motioned for Maggie to sit down on one of many folding chairs against the wall, draped with purses and bags, clothing, and shoes. The dozen female dancers moved to their own choreography. Peering out the huge warehouse window, the Hudson River slid by. Taking in the rest of the loft, Maggie noticed what must be a bathroom, a small kitchen near the door, and above it, a loft. The only other object she saw was a folding screen in the corner, which she guessed was her room.

"How nice of you to drop off your application in person."

"Thank you for seeing me," Maggie said. "After spending so much time on the application, I wanted to meet you in person and see Westbeth."

"What are those beautiful flowers on your face?"

Maggie shied. "I paint them sometimes the way women put on make-up before going out. I'm visiting a friend in the hospital this afternoon, someone who has been like a father to me. Buttercups are his favorite flower."

"I see," she said, nodding. "They are very delicate. I thought they were tattoos."

"No, they are painted on a substance made from seaweed, so at the end of the day, I can wet the edge and peel them off."

"Brilliant," said Ginger, clapping her hands. Her eyes searched the room as if to find her words. "They are… are… like an announcement…that you feel good about yourself." She laughed loudly and took Maggie's hand in hers. "My question is, can you cook?"

"Yes. I cook."

"Wonderful! Can you use computers? Answer phones? Pay bills? These are my nightmares. I need someone to help me organize."

"I am experienced in all of the above. And I'm familiar with this music, too. My mother plays John Cage's 'Concerto in B Flat' before she writes or performs. It helps her loosen up."

"How interesting. What kind of music does she play?"

"Jazz. And she sings. Her group is called the 3Ms. A female trio. I'll send you her latest CD."

"Oh, you are a darling."

The dancers rested on the floor as the music ended. They drank from thermoses. Some lay flat and stretched with arms above their heads. Others stripped naked and began putting on street clothes. Maggie was surprised to see that one was male.

Ginger leaned in: "Benje identifies as female. He fits right in."

Maggie nodded and handed off the application. "When will you make a decision on the fellowship?"

"After Labor Day. Did you have any other questions?"

"Yes. The application didn't ask about my dance experience. I have seven letters of recommendation, but when it comes to dance, I'm limited. I earned a brown belt in tae kwon do in sixth grade, and I grew up dancing in Woodstock hippie circles, little children and old people all together, but that's about it."

"You are a very lucky young woman, Ma-Gee."

Maggie had a good feeling as she closed the door. She loved the way Ginger pronounced her name with the accent on the second syllable, like Ginger's own last name, as if they were cousins. She nodded hello to a young black woman she passed on the landing. Looking through an open door, she noticed a painting studio. Big canvases everywhere. On the second floor, she heard a drum roll. The building lived and breathed art.

The next stop was on Sixth Avenue, where Maggie purchased her long-awaited phone, the bestselling Nokia 6160. She used her new credit card and set up monthly payments for a total of nine hundred dollars. Like her driver's license, she deemed the phone and credit card necessary to living on her own. Her permanent address, for now, was Carol's parent's house.

The hospital visit with Stevie was brief. After a hug, he shook his head, gave her his seat, and left the room. *He'd likely sat there since the early morning*, she thought. The seat was hot.

"Hello, Lefty. It's Maggie." She took his hand. His eyelids moved as if he was making an effort to open them but couldn't. "I came into New York with Rip. I've been staying in his mother's studio since Julia and the twins moved to California. I've got a two-month gig at Bard researching icons. You're not going to believe it, but I was walking around Rhinebeck with Rip the other day, and I got the stigmata! One big round drop of blood on my palm and a smaller one on my forehead. Please tell me the scientific reason for it. It wasn't bird shit or a dead frog, and it wasn't God. I can't even mention it to anyone except you, as people will think I'm nuts." She took a long gulp from her water bottle.

"Want a sip of water, Lefty?" He didn't answer, so she rubbed some water on his lips with her finger. "I'm still in love with Rip. He's kind and smart, like you, Lefty. It feels good like you said it would. Rip's mother calls me Juliette, which is sweet. I like that. Carol's dad called me a revolutionary, in the best sense of the word. You'd approve of that description, right? Was that the vision you had, raising me up? When you taught me to listen to the stream?"

Lefty's mouth opened, and this time, she held a cup to his lips. "Just a little taste," she said. "I don't want to drown you. Can you swallow?" She dabbed his chin and neck with a tissue. "Oops. I hope it doesn't give you a chill."

"It's such good news that Agnus is home. I bet she surprised you! I didn't remember her at first, but we've become friends.

She's beautiful, kind and smart. I see why you fell in love with her. She's going to take good care of your goats, Lefty." As soon as Maggie said this, she remembered they were sold, but she kept on. "Your goats are missing you. Everyone's planning a welcome home party for you with plenty of your favorite foods over at Old Red. Arthur and Kate. Stevie and Fern. Carol and Agnus. And Bobby and his dad. Remember them from the BBQs we used to have? Who else shall we invite?"

She was not making much sense, but Lefty's lips began moving. Maggie leaned in to hear what he said.

"Karma."

"Karma," she repeated. "You used to say *Karma is the cycle of cause and effect, the actions and the consequences of action.*"

His eyes opened to clear pools of gray. He pointed to his cheek and tried to smile.

"Yes, I painted buttercups for you, Lefty. So here's the big question I've been saving for you. Ready?"

Lefty's eyelids fluttered.

"You don't have to answer. Just listen. I've given up on finding my sperm donor. Before Julia left for California, she told me he was dead. But she told me something even better than finding him. That the two of them fell in love. That I'm a *real* love child, Lefty. My biological father wasn't just a sperm donor. That makes me feel good. Even if my parents couldn't raise me together, they loved each other. There must have been a good reason, like he was married or had taken some other kind of vow. I think a lot of adults in Woodstock know him, but everyone has promised not to tell me. It's impressive that no one has spilled the beans. One day I'll ask Stevie if you think that's okay."

Maggie didn't see Lefty's eyes close, lost as she was in her monologue. But it was time to go. She touched his cheek. "Thanks for loving me as your daughter, Lefty. I should have known better than to look for my biological father because you were always there for me. That's what I came here to say, Lefty. My love for you burns into infinity."

When Maggie arrived home that night, she read through the pages of her first week of research, picked the top ten, and sent the list off to Gertrude. The results looked measly, especially after days of hard work sleuthing the internet. And it was three days late. She apologized for missing work Monday, briefly explained Lefty's condition, and promised to make up the eight hours on Saturday.

WEEK ONE: 1. The Blue Marble. The 1972 photograph taken by Apollo 17. Earth in the universe, free of all moral judgment. 2. The Peace Sign (both the raised two fingers and the three-pronged circle) 3. A deciduous tree with branches and roots. Represents air, water, earth, the four seasons, health, life. 4. Anna Magdalena Bach, mother of 13, composer, performer, singer, teacher, transcriptionist, and aesthetic terrorist who lived uncompromisingly for art and died in a pauper's grave. 5. Shakespeare and the painting of him with a bald pate, his plays, poems, and sonnets. 6. The Cross. A negative icon. This Christian symbol seems to control a very large part of the world. A murdered human hanging on a wooden cross seems a primitive scare tactic with its violence. 7. The Milky Way, the visible fabric of time and space, a map of where we live. 8. The Mushroom Cloud. A negative icon, reminding us that humans can destroy all living creatures. 9. Virgin and Child (the multitude of paintings), reinforcing woman's role on earth as mother, both celebrating and limiting women's power. 10. The Statue of Liberty, a gift of friendship between the US and France, representing freedom, welcoming all seeking asylum. Unfortunately, many Americans do not agree that all humans have a right to a homeland.

Gertrude's next two assignments came in together: Create a list of your top ten American icons and a list of your top ten Female icons. Again, both seemed to Maggie too simple for a week's worth of work, but she did just that, creating fifty pages of notes at the end of two weeks. Without editing but simply highlighting her top ten in each category, Maggie clicked, and it all landed in Gertrude's inbox. She crawled into bed beside Rip, who was deep in sleep in his own bed for a change. Glancing at her small portrait hanging above the bed where Jesus on the cross once hung, she smiled and shut her eyes.

TWENTY-ONE

CAROL CAME by Bard College library with a picnic lunch as planned, and Maggie threw her arms around her. Walking over to the president's lawn, they took in the view of the rolling blue Hudson and the green Catskills looming on the other side. Hanging out with her best friend was a much-needed recharge. Maggie appreciated Joan's touch, too—the elegant picnic consisting of a small quiche, kale salad, peanut butter cookies, and iced tea. The family blanket and basket, even the thermos, metal dishes, and cutlery, were familiar and made Maggie feel like part of their family.

"How's my Millstream? In my dreams, I still sing its song," said Maggie.

"How's the lover boy who stole you from your Millstream?"

Maggie laughed. "I took the train to the city with him yesterday to deliver the fellowship application. Fingers crossed, Carol. Ginger and her dance company would be an exciting place to land. And Westbeth is within walking distance to your NYU dorm. Just imagine if we both live in the Village!"

"That's love," Carol said. "On another note, I'm writing another fifteen-minute Shakespeare pageant. Are you up for

Ophelia? I want her to be strong, not mentally ill—that's just something Shakespeare insinuated. It's too easy. And she's wise about Nature, including water. No drowning."

"Okay." Maggie nodded, swigging cold green tea. "Who are you playing?"

"Shakespeare, the narrator. It's *Shakespeare on Hamlet*. He interrupts actors performing key scenes."

"Love it!" Maggie said. "When is it going to happen? There isn't much summer left."

"The last weekend in August, if we can squeeze it in."

"Have you asked Stevie to do the video?"

"He hasn't returned my calls. I still need to secure five actors."

"What about Agnus?" Maggie said. "She did a few movies in Hollywood and lots of theater."

"Good idea."

Maggie took a bite of quiche. She savored the creamy custard and buttery crust as it melted in her mouth. "Mmm. Thank Joan for her yummy quiche." Maggie said, finishing a piece off.

"I gotcha!" Carol winked.

"You made it?"

"It's my summer goal. I'm learning to cook ten dishes, including your spinach lasagna."

Tossing the grapes in the air, they tried to catch them in their mouths and ended up eating them off the grass. They washed down the peanut butter cookies with the iced tea.

"Have you heard the latest on Lefty?"

"He's in recovery, right?"

A pang of loneliness shot through Maggie. With Julia and the twins gone, Rip and Carol are gone soon, and now Lefty is going. "He took a turn for the worse," Maggie said. "We are his daughters, Carol. Let's visit him together if we can find a time that works. I need to make an appointment to meet with the collector, Charlie Kim, too. He bought *eighteen* of my portraits at the library show."

"Let's do it." Carol wiped her hands on a cloth napkin. "I forgot to ask. Who won the library contest?"

"Believe it or not, Pilar—the artist I sewed for in Kingston. I don't understand how she knew Arthur and Kate… and Stevie? And you? Well, Stevie picked me up one day, so she met him."

"I remember her. A Frida Kahlo type with a long full skirt. She introduced herself to me at the opening. Strong as an oak tree."

"Yep. I'll have fun with her portrait. She has great costumes. I wonder how she'll pose."

"Do you think she'd let us borrow clothes for *Hamlet*?"

Maggie nodded. She picked up her bag. "I bet so. I've got to get back to work."

They hugged and walked off in opposite directions. Maggie paused under the shade of a tree. They'd been sitting in the sun; her neck and face felt burned. But looking deep into the green leaves, she closed her eyes. "I love you, Carol!" Maggie called.

Carol turned and waved.

Maggie ran up the one flight of stairs and settled back at her cubicle with a view of the tennis courts. The happy sound of the balls hitting the court made her feel close to Rip, who continued to play on weekends even as he remained enthusiastic about architecture. Turning on her computer, Gertrude dropped the bomb.

"Here it is," she wrote. "Now you are prepped for your final assignment. Work on it for your remaining five weeks and see what you come up with. It's a biggy. Take a deep breath. I want cultural habits, customs, and beliefs throughout history that stole women's power. How did anti-women beliefs normalize in a culture? Follow your intuition. It will be like learning to read all over again. It may mean rewriting history."

"Shit," Maggie said out loud. Her heart began to race as she opened up the Book of Genesis. The next time she looked out the window, it was 5:00 p.m. She was still writing about the framing of Eve's story, blaming her for the downfall of humanity, therefore justifying the need for men to rule over women. But Eve must have seen Eden as a walled garden; that knowledge was a good thing, and knowledge freed Adam and Eve. The snake, only natural in a garden, had been turned into a phallic symbol by outside forces, turning Eve and the snake's relationship into an adulterous affair and Eve into a fallen woman. Because of Eve's power, fear of female sexual power rose like a monster in the minds of men. By the end of the week, Maggie had spent a day on each of the following:

- The Chinese practice of lotus feet from the 10th century to 1949. Girls were crippled "to make better wives" by breaking their toes, folding and binding them to the bottom of their feet, and disabling them. Unable to "wander" or run away, all they could do was sit and sew, which brought in money for the family.
- The ancient Roman Vestal Virgins. Small girls were taken from their families to serve a restricted, ritualistic lifestyle. If any "impurity" or complaints occurred, one or two were killed in a sacrificial cleansing. It was said to be an "honor" to be a Vestal Virgin. The lucky ones were freed after serving thirty years.
- The practice of Female Genital Mutilation: hundreds of millions suffer from the practice in 30 countries. Girls from infancy to age 15, in the name of, again, making "better wives." A daughter with FGM brings in a better price in marriage.

- "Witches" in Europe and America were drowned or burned to death in the seventeenth and eighteenth centuries because of superstitious fears of women's powers, their strange looks, or "illnesses."
- The Magdalene Laundries, from 1759 to modern times, enslaved pregnant, unmarried women in England, Ireland, the US, Canada, and Australia, often for life. Many of the babies were killed, and many women died in childbirth or while still young.

"What about the men?" Maggie asked aloud in the library when she came across the 1918 public health program called the Chamberlain-Kahn Act or the American Plan: the federal government's plan to combat the spread of venereal disease by incarcerating women. Many states still have this law on the books.

Maggie ignored the students who looked up at her from their various computer terminals. It was only mid-week, but she sent off a note to Gertrude:

I started with Genesis. Eve's story was a declaration of war between the sexes. I've come upon five or six cultural traditions that maim women from China, Kenya, England, and the U.S. The worst part is that mothers and grandmothers are complicit in many of the tortures. I don't have evidence, but it seems like the invention of war, whenever that was, divided humans into warriors and breeders of warriors. How are we going to gain control of our bodies, our voices, and our finances after all these centuries of losing? Starting with Genesis is like starting in the middle of a story. What came before?

Rip had a fundraiser in the city and wouldn't get into Rhinecliff until 11:00 that night. Maggie worked until eight, then swam laps at the Bard pool. As she pulled her bikini from her backpack, the distinct smell of the Millstream made her smile. She showered and then selected one of the two open lanes, put on her goggles, and dove in. Alternating between the freestyle and breaststroke, swimmers slipped by her like tropical fish in a blur of color and bubbles as she pulled herself through the water. She remembered an article about whale songs: that if a whale off Florida sang at noon, a whale off Nova Scotia would hear the song at twelve forty. She thought about how magnificent it was that Carol's parents swam around the world. She'd like to do that. And travel the silk road from Italy to China, tasting dumplings along the way. Maggie was impatient to know the world for herself through her five senses.

She rinsed in the shower and toweled off in front of the mirror, noticing that at sixteen, she still hadn't developed much curve; her hips were mostly bones. The swim tired her out, and she felt like she drove in slow motion to Rhinebeck. Rummaging around in the Jorgenson refrigerator, she settled on a little glass container of vanilla yogurt, some crackers, and snap peas from Gertrude's garden. She ate at the kitchen table, then settled back in an Eames chair in the living room with a book from the lower level of the coffee table, a collection of essays by Gerrit Jorgensen from 1965 to 1982. Rip's father! Starting at the end of the book with his last article, "Where Have All the Women Gone," she read about Sylvia Plath, winner of The Pulitzer Prize for her *Collected* Poems—the only female winner that year. She kept her eye on the time as she read a couple of other essays, then turned to Gertrude's introduction. It included their meeting in a freshman drawing class at Brown.

"I'm afraid I stink," Rip said when she met him on the train platform at 11:00.

Sniffing his shirt, she guessed: "Alcohol, red meat, sweat." His hair, usually cut short, had grown over his ears and down his neck since deciding against pursuing professional tennis. "You taste like a wild animal."

He kissed her behind her ear. "And you're salty."

"Yep. I prefer it to chlorine. I swam thirty-five laps at the Bard pool after work." She climbed into the driver's seat of the Honda, buckled her seatbelt, and pulled out into traffic: "How was your event?"

"I've tagged along to mother's fundraisers since kindergarten, so they usually aren't much fun. But tonight happened to be the kind I like, with board members, parents, kids, movie stars, and politicians acting silly—singing and dancing a madcap little musical narrated by Sir somebody or other with an Irish brogue. They seem to have exceeded their goal to raise a million dollars for kids on the spectrum." Rip leaned back against the headrest. "I wrote my check and left half an hour early to catch the nine o'clock train. How was your day, honey?"

Maggie laughed. She hadn't heard him use that line before.

They woke in the middle of the night to the outdoor light popping on. The curtains had been left open in the studio since a stone wall surrounded the garden. It was a lumbering black bear in all her loping girth and grace, waltzing among the apple trees. Surprise! She came up to their dark window as if attempting to peer in! And a baby bear waddled up behind her! Maggie and Rip huddled naked under their sheet as the bear delicately plucked immature apples from the branches.

"I skimmed the book of your father's articles. His interests broadened and deepened over the decades—art and literature, politics, prison reform, urban poverty, women's rights. I wish I could have met him. Gertrude's introduction is a beautiful love story. What shocked me was that not only was your father a feminist, but your grandfather was also a feminist. You are a rare breed, Rip."

He smiled. "Mother said that putting the book together helped her get through the first years after his death. She sent me to a shrink when I was five, and I told him a cartoon dream I had. My father was forced to eat something out of a can, like Popeye. Not spinach and not poison, but something heavy. With each can he ate, he sank deeper into the earth until his feet poked through the other side of the planet and he floated out into space. Looking back, I'm grateful to the therapist. He just listened and accepted my story as factual. Death was never scary after that."

TWENTY-TWO

CAROL AND MAGGIE went their separate ways when they arrived in New York. Maggie headed to Charlie Kim's at the end of East 72nd Street. She planned to join Carol at the hospital after her meeting. Charlie talked for more than two hours about growing up in New Jersey, wanting to be a rock n' roll star, attending City College, and finding his way to Woodstock in 1969. The festival, he said, was like an alarm clock going off. Afterward, he gave up music for finance. When he made his first million, he bought a Durer at auction and his first Kiki Smith sculpture at a fundraiser. At Charlie's first pause, he walked Maggie to the corner of his living room where her eighteen portraits hung over his grand piano. The shadow of sun wrestling in the leaves of a tall indoor plant played over her paintings, highlighting details of the tiny flowers, birds, and butterflies in some of the paintings. Maggie pointed to a portrait of Arthur with a bee on his nose and laughed. Charlie moved in close as he hadn't noticed the bee before. For Maggie, the portraits represented blood relatives. The Woodstock mantra of *peace and love* shined through.

"It's a beautiful arrangement," Maggie said.

"I've learned to trust my instinct—I should have bought more of Kiki's work when she was starting out. We didn't know each other back in New Jersey, but I watched her career evolve."

Maggie followed Charlie into the kitchen and took a stool at the counter while he brewed tea. He produced a platter of pastel cookies, and she nibbled one that was mauve-colored, sucking on the sweet paste as it dissolved on her tongue. This occupied her. She didn't feel compelled to make conversation. Her mind wandered to Lefty. She hoped Stevie would stay with Carol rather than running out as he did when she visited.

"Do you play the piano?" Maggie asked.

"I played with your mother a bit, but she had talent. I was merely having fun posing as a musician."

Back in the living room with their tea, Charlie turned the pages of Maggie's notebooks for almost forty-five minutes. She sat next to him on the couch, her legs crossed, answering his occasional questions as she gazed at the other art hanging in the living room. A marble bust on a side table looked like a saint, her eyes heavenward, and her beautiful marbled hair raked into a bun on her neck. A very large abstract gray and black painting with subtle lines of yellow and turquoise hung above the saint. A fiber piece made of old Kimonos and a glass collection shimmered opposite her own work.

"I like these drawings of eyes," he said.

"I have twin siblings. A girl and a boy, otherwise I would call them identical. I drew their eyes until I could see them differently."

"And I'm curious about this." He lifted the notebook to show her the newest pages filled with cartoons followed by a Venn diagram, intersecting circles, a five-pointed star, and a sidebar scribbled with words.

"I'm working on a project this summer for Gertrude, Lulu's friend, having to do with icons."

He nodded and closed the last notebook, placing it on top of the others on the coffee table. "Is it Gertrude's son that you are dating?"

Maggie nodded.

Charlie hesitated. "I don't know if Julia made it clear to you, but I am your biological father, Maggie. I'd like us to know each other."

Maggie was startled by his comment. Her ears burned. Emergency! Emergency! Mistrust was her next reaction, then disappointment. He lured her to his apartment as an art dealer. That he was in possession of eighteen of her portraits now made her queasy. It was as if buying her work was a form of paternal support. That he considered her nothing but a "girl" in the worst sense of the word. The whole thing felt like a pat on her head. As if he was saying, *good girl* to a dog. Like he considered her good enough to claim as his own.

Maggie sat up straight on the couch, uncrossed her legs, and yanked the rubber band out of her hair. Unleashing her ponytail, she shook out the tight curls until they surrounded her face like Medea's snakes. She wanted him to see how different she was from him. It gave her calm as she gathered her words.

"Before Julia left for California, she informed me that my biological father was dead."

Now Charlie pulled back. He had been expecting a family reunion. Reconciliation. A relationship. A grateful embrace with a public announcement to follow. He shook his head, covered his face with his hands, and laughed. Maggie packed up her notebooks and walked out of the meeting.

Carol and Maggie hitched a ride back to Woodstock with Stevie. It had been decided that Agnus would look after Lefty for two more nights, then Stevie would be back to relieve her. She, Stevie, and Carol had not been together in Stevie's truck since he drove them to the abortion clinic. Now Maggie sat in the middle as they headed to Big Deep, a swimming hole in the woods where they could strip naked. They were in need of a real soak. Maggie remembered Carol's book of gynecological herbs women distributed among themselves in ancient times. She wanted to borrow the book again for her research. She needed to read the ancient plays.

"How was your meeting with Charlie Kim?" Carol asked.

"I'm not enthralled."

"But it's fantastic to have a collector, Maggie. It's huge. Don't shrug it off," Carol said.

Stevie chimed in. "He's investing in you."

She dunked her head under the stream and counted to ten. When she came up, Rip had arrived in his tennis whites. Like one of the ancient river gods, he unceremoniously removed his clothes and dipped his athletic body into the Millstream. He and Maggie entwined comfortably beneath the water. Looking up, Maggie saw Carol and Stevie's stunned faces. They finally glimpsed his formal beauty, exuding the Greek trifecta of freedom, confidence, and humility. Carol would never again hold a grudge against her for loving Rip. His every movement seemed true and exact. Never rushing, never flustered. Maggie herself long ago had vowed to emulate him, to glide through the world like a work of art, purposeful, with sensitivity. Without assumptions. Without wasting time or thought.

The following week, Maggie made it over to Pilar's sewing loft to sketch the portrait she owed her. The beautiful tapestries had been shipped off to Albany. The walls were bare; hence the sunlight shining off them was super bright. As Maggie prepared her pencils and brushes, watercolors, and easel, Pilar stepped out of her jeans and t-shirt, her black hair swinging down to her waist. "What color would you like?" Pilar called.

"You pick. I'm going to do a quick sketch today. I'll use that to make your oil painting. I can probably have it for you by next week."

"There's no rush."

"But I need to finish it before moving to the city," Maggie said. "By the way, Pilar. Tell me how you happened to correctly name all my people?"

Her laugh burst forth. "If you recall, we talked through our many hours of sewing together. You must have described everyone you know. And they were all at the opening. I recognized them and introduced myself. I guess I just put two and two together."

"You even got Loretta, who protests war every Sunday on the green, and she wasn't even there!"

"That was luck. I recognized her portrait. We were in a book group together when our kids were little."

"I'm so glad you won."

Maggie watched Pilar parade as if on a runway, hips out in front, sashaying purposefully across the studio in a deep purple floor-length dress. She turned, dramatically displaying her bare back. She placed a black fascinator upon her head, its tulle covering her eyes, its odd angles sticking up on top like a poisonous flower.

"The dress is from a theater company in Lenox, Mass. Modern and ancient. That's me, right? The hat is a gift I received years ago from a Parisian designer and, shall I say, a much younger lover."

Maggie situated a side view of Pilar in the light streaming from the window and lifted her long hair over her right shoulder so it hung down like a horsetail. "I'd like to paint you in profile —your nose, throat, and breast as one curvaceous line—and your bare back as one luminous plane of flesh. What do you think?"

"Sure."

Ribbons of pencil appeared on Maggie's paper as she struggled to find the lines she wanted. A forehead cut by the hat, nostrils wide, and chin rounded. The overcast sky darkened, and Maggie switched on a standing lamp. She picked up a flat, broad bush and, with one stroke, painted Pilar's bare back, then added a wash of pink, gray, and yellow.

"What's your favorite flower?" Maggie asked. "Arthur, my first art teacher, taught me to love nature. To honor him, I like to include some bit of nature in my portraits."

"Red rose."

Maggie handed Pilar a pincushion. "Let's pretend this is the rose. Hold it right below your breasts."

Driving to the train station to pick up Rip, she remembered Pilar quoting Louise Bourgeois: *Each stitch is an act of repair.* Humans need constant repair from cultural lies, prejudice, and pain. She was grateful that Julia lied about her father's death: it was ammunition. Without it, how would she have countered Charlie Kim's fake claim? Maggie needed to sift through past conversations with her mother for other useful bits of information.

Waiting for Rip on the train platform in Rhinecliff, Maggie punched in her mother's number and left a message. "I visited Lefty. He is very weak, but we had a nice long chat. Or, I should say, I had a nice long monologue with him. He opened his eyes and said a total of one word: karma. Of all words, it was a gift to me. I thought about the sum of his life determining his future—does he really believe in future lives? He pointed to the buttercups on my face, and that was it. Call me."

TWENTY-THREE

"MS. JAMES?" Maggie called, knocking at her office door. She heard James talking on the phone, so she wandered into the art section of the library to wait. It was extensive for a small town. Her favorite book to browse, *Michelangelo, Divine Draftsman and Designer,* was too big to ever check out and carry home, so over the years, she had returned to it. Remembering Charlie Kim's interest in the page of eyes in her notebook, she searched for Michelangelo's exercise sheet drawn by master and students. She liked the oval shapes, the iris, and the small pearl-like shape in the corner of the eye. Again, she took out her notebook. Somehow, Rip's eyes set deep between his strong brow and nose always ended up looking angry when she certainly didn't see him that way. A side view was easier, but she wanted to capture him straight on. Lost in the moment, she remembered this was her lunch hour. She had to get back to Bard. Thanks to Gertrude's car, she could be back in her cubicle with a snap of her fingers. All those wet days walking the twins home from school, all the bundling and unbundling to warm them up with cocoa or cool them down with homemade popsicles, came to her. She knocked again on Ms. James' door.

"Come in," Ms. James called.

"Hi. I'm here to pick up the painting of my mother."

"Oh, Maggie. What a nice surprise." Ms. James rummaged in a deep desk drawer and handed over a brown paper package with Maggie's name on it.

"Do you have a personal icon?" Maggie asked as she removed the bubble wrap and leaned back in the chair.

Ms. James lifted the framed photograph on her desk and turned it around. "My horse, Blackjack. Why do you ask?"

"Beautiful," Maggie whispered. She set the photo back on Ms. James' desk. "I'm doing a project for Gertrude Jorgensen. Do you know her?"

Ms. James shook her head.

"She's a sculptor at Bard who hired me for eight weeks. She says she hired me because I'm in the first quintile, growing up without television." Maggie now held up the painting of Julia, cracking a smile. "I see this painting of my mother differently now that we don't live together."

Ms. James nodded: "Yes. Perspective changes with time."

"Waking to my mother's nightly escapades really skewed things for me."

"What do you mean?" Ms. James asked.

"She always came in around two in the morning after a gig. I'd wake up and concentrate on the sounds of the Millstream, but every night ended up trying to figure out who she brought home." Maggie stuck the painting into her backpack and jumped up. "Oops! I've got to go—it's my lunch hour. Uh, I'd still like to take you up on your offer to visit your ranch sometime and learn to ride a horse."

"Oh!" she laughed. "That would be great. But I will warn you; if you sleep above the barn, Blackjack makes lots of noises in the night."

Maggie smiled and gave her a thumbs-up.

The following day, news arrived via Agnus that Lefty had died peacefully in his sleep. By evening, more than fifty people had gathered at Old Red, bearing watermelon, rice and beans, chicken, fish, whatever anyone had in their fridge. Stevie brought the last of Lefty's specialty from the freezer—homemade banana-chocolate goat's milk ice cream. Maggie painted buttercups across her face again and made Lefty's favorite dipping sauces for the grilled meats and vegetables—spicy Thai peanut, Chinese mustard, and a Peruvian green sauce. Musicians played, dancers linked arms, and a line snaked around the house, looping the barn and cottage and past the swimming hole where kids and adults jumped in with or without clothes. A bonfire burned, colorful strings of Christmas lights were plugged in, and blankets spread under the stars. Stevie told the story of hiking all thirty-five peaks in the Catskills with his dad and once when he was twelve, getting caught in a three-day snowstorm on Slide Mountain. They huddled in sleeping bags and sang songs as snow piled around their tent. Kate talked about Lefty driving twelve of them in Old Red's magic school bus to Mexico one summer and when it broke down, living for three months in a small mountain village teaching English, learning Spanish, and figuring out how to fix the transmission. Someone else remembered a time on Fire Island when Lefty saved a kid from drowning. Maggie added that Lefty attempted to teach her goat language. She posted her drawings of him in the living room next to Arthur's photographs. Stevie opened *The Exquisite Corpse* to Lefty's dragon, which always spooked him as a kid because it looked so human. Carol, Fern, Rip, Stevie, and several others gathered around the bonfire, drinking and smoking until near midnight. After Maggie helped clean the kitchen, she found Rip and told him that she was ready to go.

That same week, Carol's mom left a message for Maggie that

Ginger from the MaGee Dance Studio wanted her to call. It wasn't until after dropping Rip off at the train station the following morning that Maggie heard the message. She called from the car in the Bard parking lot, but Ginger didn't pick up. All day, the possibility of good news distracted her from fully concentrating. Finally, at nearly five o'clock, they connected.

"Ma-Gee!" Ginger's jolly voice rang out. "I've selected you for the two-year fellowship and mailed a contract. Please read through the materials carefully, sign, and return the contract as soon as possible. Let me know if you have any questions. I look forward to working with you, darling."

The news energized Maggie. Over the next week, she worked diligently, pulling together not an essay or a formal research paper but sixty pages of carefully annotated notes on her last five weeks of research. She handed the notes to Gertrude's computer assistant, Lael, and asked for feedback.

"What do you think?" Maggie asked when she ran into her in the cafeteria. They hadn't had a real conversation since the first day they met. "I mean, it's just the beginning. Imagine if women from every country wrote about their cultural history of silencing women. That's what we need to document the problem."

"It's fucking depressing," Lael said. "That's why I stick to computer science."

"Did you read it?"

"I skimmed most of it. I don't understand how it will help."

"The purpose is to create a path toward a solution. And educate the public."

Maggie finished her cup of coffee and went back to her computer terminal to write a thank you to Gertrude. After sending off the whole package, she headed back to the Rhinebeck studio to pack and clean up. Saturday, Rip drove her to Carol's house. Without ceremony, they kissed goodbye as they had many times. They agreed to stay in touch but didn't have any immediate plans. Maggie was still high from the fellowship acceptance, oblivious to the pain she'd experience once he left for college.

TWENTY-FOUR

"SHE LOVES ME, YEAH, YEAH, YEAH," Maggie sang into the phone. "Stevie, are you there? I got my fellowship in the city!"

"On my way to work," Stevie said.

"Come by Carol's after, and I'll make you dinner to celebrate. I have the house to myself for a week while Carol's parents are in New York. Also, if you have any more small oak boards, could you save them for me?"

"I've got a few around here. I'll toss them in the truck."

Without a car to drive at every whim, time slowed way down. The weather was hot and muggy, typical of an East Coast summer day. After lunch, she dipped into the stream to cool down and then headed to the garage in her wet bikini. She wanted to paint a family portrait of Lefty, Agnus, and Stevie, but instead, she started on a second painting of Rip—this one to keep for herself. She struggled with his bare upper torso and turned to the studies she made while pursuing Arthur's big fat *Atlas of Human Anatomy and Surgery*. Using the point of the brush like a pen, she outlined Rip's torso, then painted in the background, adding her own tiny portrait on the wall above his right shoulder. She knew she'd have to return to Rip several times to get him right, but when complete, she planned to hang it in her room at Ginger's.

After cleaning up the oil paints, she called Ginger to ask how much space there was between the bed and the screen. She wanted to bring a table for her computer. Ginger went to take measurements and, finally, after more than ten minutes, returned to the phone.

"There's eighteen inches between the bed and the wall. And by the way, in case you need more storage space, I have a room in the basement where you can store things."

"Oh, perfect," Maggie said.

Stevie showed up depleted after his shift at the hardware store. She took his hand and led him to the stream. Still in her bikini, she dunked again to cool off while he soaked his feet. His father's death had worn him thin.

"Any offers on Lefty's place?"

"Not yet. But Agnus' offer on the Glasco Turnpike house was accepted. It's near the four corners, a good location for me. I can take the bus to New Paltz if I don't like dorm living."

"Are you excited about college?"

"No. Fern and I broke up."

"What?"

"I'm not much fun to hang with these days."

"You're in mourning, Stevie. Give yourself a break."

"Do you not want me to be honest?"

She hesitated. Their usual silence together didn't feel like old times. Finally, she spoke. "I have a big question for you. Because you *are* honest. I feel like a lot of people around town know who my father is, and I'm wondering if you do."

His eyes locked on hers. "I do. I know him well. I've seen him a few times since Lefty died. He's got a good understanding of things."

Maggie's face was beaming. "Julia told me he was dead, but I didn't believe her."

"She said it for a good reason," Stevie said. "To keep him safe."

"But I'm his grown daughter. Why can't I know him?"

"Let it be, Maggie. And be glad because he knows and loves you."

Maggie had to keep her mouth shut now. She relished the news as she mashed avocados for guacamole and poured corn chips into a bowl and salsa into a smaller bowl. She heated leftover rice and beans and grated cheese. They decided to chill with a half-drunk bottle of rose left in Carol's parents' fridge—she'd leave five bucks on the window sill. Around midnight, they took a walk through town and stood outside what would soon be Agnus' new house, a wooden two-story bungalow set back off the road with a huge swath of tall pink cosmos dancing with fireflies. Maggie and Stevie hooted and hollered as they walked the dark road, recounting some of their younger escapades, like cross-dressing, skipping school when Stevie was in fifth grade and Maggie in third, and sneaking out to sleep in their treehouse behind Old Red. Last but not least was the striptease Maggie and Carol performed for him.

"How could I forget that," Stevie said. "That's when I fell in love with Carol."

"So you've been in love with her a long time. Are you going to study film in college?"

He shrugged. "I slept with Carol again; that's why Fern broke up with me."

It was past 2:00 a.m. when they flopped down on the couch at Carol's. "You can sleep in Carol's bed tonight. I'll take the couch. Just bring me a blanket from her room. And by the way, I bought a book about writing screenplays. I'm thinking about writing a piece called *Taking Off*—a brother and sister in search of their father. They get into scrapes and meet scary, weird people."

"I like it," he said.

"I'll send you a draft once I get started."

Maggie was still asleep when Rip called the next morning. She opened her eyes and saw that it was 9:30. Stevie was already back at the Hardware store.

"I talked to the dean of admissions," he said. "I can pre-register for classes and skip freshman orientation, but I had to promise to try out for the tennis team. And I arranged to leave two days early at the architecture firm. That gives me four free days. So I booked us tickets to Paris. We leave in three days. I assume you have a valid passport?"

"What? Yes! I renewed it a couple of years ago when I traveled to Berlin with Julia's trio. So, we're going to Paris?"

"Just three nights. I used my points for the plane tickets, so there's no air cost. Splitting food and hotel shouldn't be more than five hundred each."

It all happened so fast. Maggie emailed Carol and her parents to let them know she was off to Paris and figured a postcard to her mother and the twins would do. Snuggling next to Rip in the plane was thrilling. Maggie didn't want to map out the future. Jumping at opportunities as they arose was just fine. That was her last thought until it was announced that they were over Ireland and would land in Paris in half an hour. After checking into their hotel, they had sex on thick white cotton sheets and slept. Rip went out and bought cheese on Rue du Bac. Farther on, he bought grapes, water, a baguette, and a chocolate bar they ate inside the bread—Rip's childhood favorite. The big windows in their room opened, and they watched school children in uniforms play in the street, then hurried off to the Louvre to peek at Da Vinci's *Mona Lisa* before closing. Rip knew his way around Paris; she held his hand, taking it all in. She especially loved the sound of the French language coming from his lips.

Reaching the Louvre, Rip straight away led Maggie to her favorite painting. She wove through the crowd to stand as close as possible. It was a mystery she wanted to solve, the Mona Lisa's secretive look—male and female, smiling and not smiling—Maggie saw her eyes rove the crowd, just as she had read about. Twenty minutes was all she had, but at closing time, she felt filled up, even exhausted. They walked the Jardin Des Tuileries until dusk and, afterward, dined at a small place in Pontoise. Rip ordered olives, asparagus, and avocado salad, a mushroom tart in cream sauce, and cake with mint sauce and pistachios.

Rip seemed decades older than her as he casually joked with waiters and the hotel concierge. She couldn't imagine a better guide to Paris or a better boyfriend. She wondered why she was letting him slip away even though they really loved each other. Putting the big questions aside, she tried to relax and observe the world around her. She found the houseboats docked along the Seine romantic and the Roman baths intriguing. The tapestries at the de Cluny were utterly and completely fantastic. Rip told her about the Unicorn tapestries at the Cloisters in New York, which she made a mental note to visit. After gazing at Notre Dame's flying buttresses and stained glass, they descended beneath the plaza to the first century. Maggie's energy wavered in the cool, damp underground air that smelled medieval. She took Rip's arm and buried her head in his side, trying not to breathe in the smell of death. He laughed. For him, archeology was a window into early architecture. He told her that as a kid, he always begged his mother to take him underground when they visited Paris.

Back on the street, they stopped for coffee and shared an apple tart before heading to the Picasso Museum, which was crowded. Maggie enjoyed a quick glance at his early portraits of thick-limbed Spaniards, his collages, cubist paintings, ceramics, and cast metal sculptures, all the while wondering how he managed as an outsider in France. She tried to imagine what new direction her art would take next. One day, she would learn to weld and perhaps make sculpture.

They walked and didn't pause until reaching the Pompidou Centre. Without time to go in, Rip gave her a heads up on the beauty of its high-tech industrial architecture, designed by a team of four: Rogers, Rogers, Piano, and Franchini. Its colorful "inside-out" structure confused her.

"I see I have some studying to do," she said when she realized it was not under construction. This was her way of admitting that she didn't appreciate its significance. Gazing through the window to a Calder sculpture, she pointed. "I like that," she said.

The next day, they returned to the Louvre now that they had time to explore. The sun touched the top of the glass pyramid and lit one triangle, so it seemed magically freestanding in the stone plaza. This time, they entered through the Sully wing and took in the four ancient Cariatides gracing the entrance. Maggie was struck by a painting of an Egyptian couple wearing leopard skins and painted fruit. Rip steered her toward the Venus de Milo goddess of Aphrodite, but Maggie moved on toward the Winged Victory above the staircase: headless, her arms carved as wings, lifting her torso toward the sky like a bird. Maggie recognized it as a physical expression of joy. They viewed paintings by Ingres, Titian, Da Vinci, Raphael, Caravaggio, Tiepolo, Guardi. This was followed by an artichoke salad and salmon with a bottle of cold white wine and chocolate parfait. Back in their room, jet lag hit them, and the very thick cotton sheets brought instant sleep.

They spent their last day walking the Luxembourg Gardens

and Montparnasse Cemetery. They took the subway to Mont Martre and Sacre Coeur: Rip dozed to the choir while Maggie was transfixed, ready to get thee to a nunnery. At sunset, they strolled along the Seine with so many lovers, drank beer, and ate Greek food in the Latin quarter.

Maggie continued to walk around Paris long after her return to Tinker Street. Gertrude and Roland were back from Morocco, suntanned and happy to be home. Rip was packing for college. The four of them had one last quick Chinese take-out dinner together, where Rip compared the details of all his many visits to Paris, emphasizing that the best was with Maggie.

She told the story of the two bears picking apples in the walled garden behind the studio. Rip, embarrassing Maggie, told of the mysterious stigmata.

Roland was amazed. Gertrude giggled.

Maggie touched Roland's arm across the table. "Please let me know when you figure out the scientific reason for it," she said. They all cleared the table, and after helping with the dishes, it was time to go. She handed off her house and car keys to Gertrude. "Thanks for everything. I really enjoyed your home these last two months."

"I'm teaching a three-day workshop at the Art Students League this fall," Gertrude said. "So we'll get together in the city to discuss your research." Then she presented Maggie with her paycheck.

Too soon, Maggie and Rip were again parked in Carol's driveway. She gave him a juicy kiss and moved to open the door, then changed her mind and struggled to climb onto his lap. He pushed the Triumph's seat back as far as it would go. She swung her legs onto the passenger seat, her face in his neck. They held tight.

"I'll miss our kissy nights," she said. "Please don't fall in love with anyone else right away, Rip. Let me linger in your heart a little while."

"I'm going to visit as soon as you settle in at the dance company."

"Okay," she said, opening the door.

TWENTY-FIVE

BLACKJACK, a sleek, long-legged stallion, pranced alone in the front pasture. Six mares grazed in the gently sloping field above, all his offspring. Four geldings, also his, roughhoused in the next field over. Blackjack chased deer, Canadian geese, and even rabbit from his pasture, but when Ms. James appeared, he snorted and pawed lustily at the earth.

Out of desperation, Maggie had put in a call to Ms. James.

"What's wrong?"

"I have a week before my fellowship starts in the city, and I was wondering if I could take you up on your offer and stay a few days above the barn. I've only ridden a horse once and want to learn. I'm happy to help with chores."

"What about your boyfriend?"

"Gone to college. Truthfully, it feels like he's been torn from me as if it ended badly when it didn't. I've actually broken out in shingles."

Ms. James groaned. "That's stress. You must have had chickenpox as a kid. Meet me at the library at six, and I'll drive you to the ranch. Cold showers help with the burning, and I have some ointment and other remedies. You are welcome to stay this week."

Maggie imagined it would be like the sleep-away camp she attended once, but this was for grownups. She learned *tout de suite* that Ms. James wasn't just a librarian interested in animal husbandry but in gambling as well. Each evening, the dining room was filled with eight plus cigar-smoking, whiskey-swilling adults, yelling and teasing, pounding the table piled with cash. They called Ms. James simply…James.

Robbie, a thin forty-year-old cowboy who reminded her of Lefty, introduced Maggie to a brown mare named Belle with a curly golden mane. He showed her how to place the saddle over the blanket, adjust the cinch and the stirrups, hold the horn, and swing her leg wide to mount her. He advised that she hold the reins firmly, neither tight nor loose. "Remember, you're the boss," he said. "Horses like to know you're the boss."

Riding the paths side by side around the fields felt to Maggie a bit like a merry-go-round, but Robbie's explanations about the workings of the ranch were entertaining. Every second day, two geldings rotated into Blackjack's pasture for equine grooming and general company, but Robbie had to keep an eye on them because they might nip or kick, and James didn't want her prize stud scarred. After two days of frolic, Blackjack spent a night in the barn to get his beauty sleep.

Toward the end of the week, Robbie took Maggie on a trail through the woods. A low-hanging pine branch knocked across her forehead as they ran up a small rise. Despite the blood, she laughed as Robbie cleaned her up in the barn's equine kitchen, where special diets and medicines were cooked for horses.

"How long have you been working for James?" Maggie asked as he applied a poultice and adhered tape over her forehead.

"My whole life, I guess," he said. "She's my older sister. The brains of the family."

After they brushed down the horses, Robbie continued, looking directly at her. "James is planning to take you on her usual ten-mile loop on Saturday, and it's my job to make sure you stay in the saddle."

Maggie was taken aback by his seriousness. "I will. I promise," she said.

Lunch was a full dinner. She ate around the meat, concentrating on mashed potatoes with butter, sautéed Brussels sprouts, and apple cinnamon cake, which Mimi baked and served with homemade ice cream. Afternoons, Maggie walked two miles down the road to a swimming hole in a stream at the end of a long, flat field. Like horseback riding, soaking naked in the stream kissed her all over, fusing body and spirit, and helped dry up the pus-filled little blisters on her torso. Maggie figured the plein air bathing was also James' cure for lovesickness mentioned in their phone call.

On a shelf back in her room, she found a book of letters between Georgia O'Keeffe and a girlfriend, documenting the challenge of painting. O'Keeffe noted how seductive it was to be praised for her art and how craving praise threw her off and made painting more difficult. Alfred Stieglitz, her lover, first exhibited her paintings and helped her break through the male New York art world. Critics wrote about her large sexualized flowers when she claimed to merely express the importance of examining nature up close. Maggie appreciated the intensity of O'Keeffe's wavy New York skyscrapers and their windows lit yellow as if her spirit glowed inside.

Returning to the stream the next day, Maggie noticed that none of the roads had signs or names, and the few houses hidden in the woods did not have mailboxes or numbers. She had never been this deep in the Catskills. The tall forest surrounding the field hid the sun: she wouldn't know which direction would take her to Woodstock if she needed to find her way home. All week, she saw not a single person or car on her walks. But floating on her back in the stream, a small yellow plane roared overhead. As she watched, the plane turned and rolled upside down. She jumped out of the stream, expecting it to crash. When it straightened and repeated the roll in the opposite direction, she laughed. It then circled over the field and landed at the far end. She quickly dressed as it taxied toward her, stopping just short of the woods. A man stepped out of the plane wearing a long black coat. He shook hands with the pilot, who then handed him a small bag, and the plane turned and taxied back in the direction it came from and roared off into the pink sky. The man in the long black coat stood at the edge of the road, looking right, then left, then right. He spun around when he heard her approach.

"Good day," he said. "Maybe you can help me. I think I'm lost."

"This is called Lew Beach."

He paused. "I was told to walk straight down the road and turn left at the first intersection. But which way is straight down the road? Both directions go straight for a long way."

"What is your destination?"

"A poker game. James invited me. I met her two weeks ago at a party in Boston."

Maggie rolled her eyes. "Then we headed in the same direction. I'm Maggie. And you must be The Man in the Long Black Coat from Dylan's song."

The man who seemed so tense began to dance, snapping his fingers. "Crickets are chirpin'; the water is high. There's a soft cotton dress on the line hangin' dry."

"Your plane somersaulted, and you fell out of the sky. That was quite a performance."

"The stunt pilot is an old friend. I don't drive, so he offered to fly me over from Boston."

They walked together in silence most of the way. His strides were long, and Maggie struggled to keep up with him. Beneath his long black coat, he wore black jeans, a white T-shirt, and boots. She figured he told her his name somewhere along the way, but his strange accent prevented her from catching it. Likewise, his collar prevented her from seeing his face full-on.

"Are you an actor, by chance?" he asked. "I'm looking to fill a major role in a film I'm directing. It takes place in the future."

"What's the plot?"

"A woman swims her house to safety when the rising tide overtakes her island."

Maggie wanted to snort but held back. "It sounds like Herzog's film, pulling a boat over a mountain. I assume it will be filmed in the safety of a pool?"

"No," he said. "In a lagoon in South Carolina."

"I see. Filled with alligators. I think I've seen that movie, too. She delivers the house, but she gets eaten."

He nodded as if she was right.

Dinner was served by the time they arrived back at the ranch. Maggie slipped up to her room with a plate of beans and rice while James got up from the table to welcome the man in the long black coat. A call to Julia was overdue, so she ate her beans listening to stories about Mick and Mia's first surfing lesson. She also learned that their big brother, Toby, left to spend his summer with his mother.

"John is committed to making a happy family," Julia said. "And I'm finding my way. I'm booked through Thanksgiving. And Rip?"

"Off at college. I'm heading into the city on Monday. Ginger's dance company is going to be interesting."

"And Agnus and Stevie?"

"Agnus has been staying with a friend in the city. Stevie and I walked by her new house on Glasco. The deal hasn't closed yet, but it'll be nice. Stevie is enrolled at New Paltz, and right now, I'm at James' place for the week, learning to ride a horse. Oops! Got to go. The poker game is about to start. I promised James I'd sit next to her for good luck."

"Ms. James?"

"Yeah. Everyone here calls her James."

Robbie still wore his cowboy hat, curled tight as a snake around the brim. Mimi, the cook, turned out to be Robbie's wife. She sat across the table from him. Next to her was Curley, with a big red beard and matching suspenders. Then, a young guy or gal, Maggie couldn't tell, named Sammy. The dealer was a handsome black man Maggie had seen earlier playing a Scott Joplin piece on the piano. Next to him sat a woman with a crew cut and sunglasses they called Granny. Shirley, the housekeeper and James' business partner circled the table with a bottle of whiskey and ice, serving anyone who wiggled their little finger. A blonde woman with false eyelashes and a low-cut blouse was last to the table. She sat between Maggie and the man in the long black coat, which he had finally taken off. He was skinny with finely drawn features, shaggy black hair, and a shadow of a beard. As red and black chips piled up, bills flew, and accusations spilled forth.

"Watch your bling," Mimi said to Robbie from across the table.

"Curley's cheating again?" Robbie said.

Curley spit: "She's bluffing, you ass."

"Go fuck yourself, Curley," Sam said.

"Shut up," said Robbie.

James interrupted the squabbling: "Just so you know, I'm playing for Maggie tonight. I want to send her off to New York City with a little extra cash tomorrow."

The blonde woman next to Maggie slipped a card from her sleeve into her hand. Realizing that Maggie saw, she stuck her tongue out. It was large and flat as a cow's and pierced with a gold stud. Maggie swallowed hard. The man in the long black coat winked at her. Assuming it was all great fun, she laid her head on the table, and when the first round finished and fresh cards dealt, she told James that she was going to bed.

"I've got some purple boots for you. Size eight," James said. "I'll set them by your door. See you at sunrise."

Maggie pulled off her bandage before going to bed. The three-inch scratch across her forehead was something she could live with. She anointed the tender pox that hadn't yet dried up with James' ointment and fell asleep wondering if James and the man with the long black coat were lovers. In the morning, the purple cowboy boots were a little loose and were extremely loud going down the stairs. Saddling Belle, she squinted into the morning light pouring through the open barn door, looking for James. Once out the door, Belle spotted Blackjack galloping over the round of a hill and took off after him. At the top of the rise, Blackjack rose on his powerful hind legs, front legs clawing the air as James stood in the stirrups. She waved her hat like the iconic TV cowboy. When the horses met up, Maggie and James paused to take in the brilliant vermillion sunrise.

"It's a ten-mile loop starting just beyond that lake," James pointed. "A well-groomed bridle trail at a good clip is about an hour's ride. Up for it?"

Maggie nodded. James opened a gate with her gloved hand, and they were off. Blackjack's elegant legs wheeled across the morning vista, now ringed by blue Catskill Mountains. Maggie got into Belle's rhythm, her loose, uncombed curls rising and falling to Belle's hooves. They looked down on clouds and blue sky reflected in a lake below, like Thomas Cole's trick of looking down at the stars. She remembered Stevie warning about the crushing pain of the very thing that gave her so much pleasure. Not just love, but beauty, like the vista in front of her, was fleeting. She'd carry Rip's love with her wherever she went, even if he wasn't hers alone. She guessed he felt the same. Then a lighter thought emerged: she forgot to ask her mother if the twins got the dog they were promised. Because it wasn't mentioned in the phone call, she guessed they hadn't.

TWENTY-SIX

MAGGIE PINNED Rip's photograph of her and the stranger on the wall above her computer in her "room" at Ginger's studio. Next to that hung a sketch of Rip their last morning at the Millstream, looking as solid as the boulder he sat on. Her small portrait of him, with her face floating above his right shoulder, now hung on the wall above her bed. They left messages for each other most days, but conversations usually happened once a week, usually while Ginger snored and Rip worked into the night on his architectural assignment. She told him about her daily sketching session of the dancers during warm-up as they worked out their choreography. Her close observation revealed not only their individual styles but also their fierce commitment to dance.

"Don't rape yourself," Ginger called, turning off the music. The dancers froze. "Martha Graham said these words to me when I was new to her studio. It means do not force yourself. Don't abuse your spirit. Move with pleasure. Be in possession of your body. Above all, please yourself."

In preparation for the rehearsal of Doris Humphrey's famous piece, *Rock Sound Earth Dance*, each dancer picked up two rocks from a pile in the corner and spaced themselves evenly across the floor. They were booked to perform at the Central Park Dance Festival, weather permitting, in early November.

"Begin," Ginger called. Together, the dancers' arms and legs stretched as far as possible, and after turning, breathing, and moving away, they returned to their rocks. On their knees, they struck rock on rock in unison, like an ancient rhythmic prayer.

"Oh, I like this dressing!" Ginger said one night as she and Maggie sat at the small white table. "Once I got so bored with my own cooking, I used blueberry yogurt on my lettuce. It wasn't bad."

"This is a Balsamic mustard vinaigrette," Maggie said. "So Martha Graham is the mother of modern dance?"

"She popularized it in America."

"*Don't rape yourself* is very strong language," Maggie said.

"Exactly what women need to hear. Women know in their gut what it means. Rape and bad sex teach women to rely on out-of-body experiences to survive. Being used becomes the norm. And pretty soon, women find themselves spiritually drowning. We need to support each other. We become strong when we create work that is authentically our own."

"So this is how you became strong?"

Ginger laughed. "I'll tell you a story, *Ma-Gee*. When I was little, my father was a guard at the Hunters Point Naval Shipyard in San Francisco, and my mother was a painter. On Sundays, we took family drives into the hills near the ocean so my mother could paint in nature. My little brother had a red ball, and he and I played catch until he got tired and laid down to nap. I practiced my ballet positions, holding his red ball. One day, I got up on my toes, my heels lifting off the ground in a pirouette, and the red ball soared out of my hands toward a brilliant golden orb. I saw two small aliens with large heads, no taller than my mother, standing in front of a spaceship. I started spinning toward it when my father called my name."

"What was it?"

"A spaceship. My father grabbed me and ran back for my mother, still absorbed in her painting and…and… her smock caught on her easel, and she tripped and rolled toward the spaceship. A door opened, and the two aliens retreated. We shielded our faces as the bright ship rocketed like a triangle straight up into the sky." Ginger sighed. "I waved goodbye as my father jammed the car into gear and rocketed back onto the highway."

"Wow," Maggie said.

"You see, my father didn't understand that dancing in the light of the spaceship was the happiest moment of my life. He threatened me to never, never, never mention what we saw to anyone. But my mother and I drove back the next day. She found her straw hat, smock, and easel, and she touched up the oil painting while I searched for my brother's red ball. I thought the spaceship might land again if I could only dance. Instead, thunder rumbled between the mountain peaks. The faster the windshield wipers swished, the slower mother drove home. I studied her oil painting on the back seat: she had not painted me and my brother in the wild blueberries but the two small people standing in front of their spaceship, lit like a yellow bonfire."

Maggie took another bite of her pasta and a sip of water, her eyes locked on Ginger. "You never told anyone?"

"Not for a long while. My mother died when I was in high school, and my father remarried soon after. His new wife loved my brother but not me. I tried to win the new mother with my dances, but my father disowned me. Without college tuition, I got a waitress job in San Francisco and joined a local dance company, which resurrected me from my father's abandonment. When my dance instructor suggested I study in New York, I bought a one-way bus ticket, and at the bottom of my suitcase was my mother's painting she had hidden away. It's up in my loft now." Ginger finished eating and drank her glass of milk. "Doris Humphrey is the grandmother of modern American dance. Isadora Duncan, too. We all have two grandmothers, right?" She laughed. "Isadora Duncan founded modern dance in Europe."

With Ginger's encouragement, Maggie eventually joined the dance warm-up the first hour of rehearsal each day. It wasn't easy. She tried to mimic the twins' sense of freedom and her own escapades with Stevie and Carol, jumping through the fiery hoop or flowing like the Millstream. And she danced to the dreamy memories of her wanderings with Rip through Paris.

One of the dancers observed Maggie and her mending basket and asked if she could sew a tear in her leotard. Other dancers brought their ragged dance costumes, and soon Maggie had a basketful of mending, and they each gave her a few bucks. Ginger introduced Maggie to her friend Spencer, who lived downstairs. For five dollars a day, she took on the task of walking his two little dogs morning and night, always holding her breath as she waited outside his loft, which smelled of his yellow hair tonic and something else, deeper and darker. Once Stevie delivered her computer, she typed a vampire story for a writer on the tenth floor at fifty cents a page and made twenty bucks.

Word spread through Westbeth that Maggie was available to run errands, do light house cleaning, and shopping. Because Ginger slept eight hours a night, Maggie had most of the daily chores completed before Ginger's 10:00 a.m. alarm went off. Bill paying, and those kinds of 'unpleasantries,' as Ginger called them, became routine for Maggie. She made a spreadsheet of income and expenses and tracked the dancers' payments. Ginger didn't leave her loft except for doctors' appointments, special performances, and her weekly trip to attend to her roof garden. Maggie took advantage of Ginger's excursions and climbed the ladder to dust the loft and change the bed sheets. Only then did it become clear that Ginger's insistence on eight hours of rest was not all spent sleeping but drawing and writing. Stacks of handwritten paper stood on a shelf next to her bed, as well as a basket of colored markers and a bag of her favorite hard lemon-flavored candies. Clothes and the colorful chiffon scarves she tied around her hair were neatly folded on shelves. Abstract art, drawn on cardboard, was tacked to the walls around her bed, like colorful dancers' skirts. Ginger's mother's painting of the spaceship was tucked into one of the many cubbies. Holding it up to the daylight, Maggie examined the aliens standing in front of a glowing triangular spaceship. Between them, the red ball levitated at their shoulders.

"I saw your mother's amazing painting when I changed your sheets," Maggie said. "The red ball levitated?"

"I don't know. It seemed to be floating. I still feel its energy pulling me into the future," Ginger said. "I feel it inside me now. When I auditioned for Martha Graham at her studio, she noticed something. 'You are a sensitive young woman,' " she said. 'Take off your necklace, darling. The human form is naturally beautiful. Now, I want you to visualize. Lift, spin, and soar across the floor. Imagine that you are a red ball.' "

"Oh, goosebumps," Maggie said.

Ginger laughed heartily. "Martha Graham saw into my soul."

Every evening Maggie and Ginger sat at the small dinner table and enjoyed their meal. As promised, Maggie hadn't made the same dinner twice so far at Westbeth. Ginger made it known that she liked variation. She also liked bread, butter, and a glass of milk with her meal. Luckily, she was satisfied with a bowl of ice cream for dessert and liked every flavor.

"Do you believe in UFOs?" Maggie asked.

Ginger breathed deeply and lifted her arms skyward, smiling. "Absolutely. I believe in the power of the universe. Humans are a tiny part of existence. Accepting the universe as my focus humbles me and gives me strength. I believe that dance is the universal language."

Maggie said: "How long will it take for me to feel like I'm truly dancing, not just trying?"

"*Ma-Gee*, dear. It's muscle learning in the beginning. Your muscles must become flexible as you explore a personal vocabulary of movement. Are you doing the stretches every day?"

"I am."

"Well then, in six months, you'll begin to feel the mind/body connection. In a year, you'll realize you'll be learning for the rest of your life. However, I could point out some wonderful vocabulary I see you using in our warm-ups. Like the way you move your wrists, freeing your hands. And the way your head rotates on your neck almost like an owl, which surprises me because your shoulders are so tense. It's like your energy overrides your muscles somehow. I'll draw you a specific routine to practice on your own. But during warmups with the company, I want you to stick to the red ball burning inside you."

TWENTY-SEVEN

JUST AS THEY DREAMED, Maggie and Carol rendezvoused most weekends in Washington Square Park with a cup of take-out coffee and were entertained by a circus of dogs, children and nannies, performance artists, and students ensconced in books and chit-chat. The weather cooled by late September, and they huddled together as gusts of leaves blew into them.

"When are you going home next?" Maggie asked.

"Not until Thanksgiving. I still talk to mom several times a week. She's having trouble adjusting to her quiet life. And Rip? Are you over him?"

"Over or under," Maggie smiled. "Either way is nice."

"Nasty." Carol smiled.

"Men are not allowed in the studio during rehearsal, so I couldn't show Rip around when he came to the city," Maggie said. "Instead, he gave me an architectural tour of lower Manhattan—the Brooklyn Bridge, crediting the engineer's wife, Emily Roebling, with completing the bridge when her husband got sick; the Woolworth building, covered in terracotta tiles outside and inside, a marble lobby and a vaulted ceiling with stained glass; Federal Hall and its bronze statue of George Washington at the top of the steps; the pointed spires of Trinity Church surrounded by an old haunted graveyard. I wanted to go to Windows on the World, but it was closed for a private party, so we took the subway to Central Park and found a dry spot in the woods for kissy kissy." She nodded to a couple embracing on the grass. "Next time, we'll book a hotel for the day if that's all we have."

"Well," Carol said. "My first night in the dorm, everyone was taking drugs and having sex."

"Impressive," said Maggie. "So you found a new girlfriend?"

"A boy from China. He said the mark on my shoulder might be a tattoo made by my birth family as a way to help me find my way home. I have to research it."

"What did Joan say?"

"She said whenever I'm ready, we'll go to China."

"Your mother is a goddess."

The following day, Maggie finally met up with Gertrude, another one of Maggie's goddesses, on the steps of The Art Student League. They walked a half block to the Carnegie Deli. It was crowded, and the waiter gruff. Maggie startled when he slammed a plate of latkes on the table, nearly toppling the small dishes of sour cream and applesauce. Luckily, he was gentler with Gertrude's matzo ball soup. Maggie nodded to Gertrude as a man at the next table tried to get his mouth around a four-inch pastrami sandwich.

"That's what this place is famous for," Gertrude said.

Maggie laughed. "How was teaching?"

"I enjoy beginners working with clay. The tactile experience brings out an unbridled curiosity in people."

"Why, then, am I so self-conscious when I join he morning dance warm-up? I'm much more comfortable watching them as I mend torn dance costumes or sketch the dancers."

"Are they all women?"

"Yes, except for one, and he fits right in. Ginger, at seventy-something, is truly amazing. She's small with a round shape, yet as limber as the twenty-year-olds. She does splits and lifts her leg to her forehead, spins at top speed, then slowly lowers onto her belly in a turtle position, her hands holding her feet, her neck and chin outstretched."

"I admire your drive to learn multiple disciplines."

It wasn't until the table was cleared and coffee ordered that Gertrude took up the topic of Maggie's research. "I don't have my notes here, but I wanted to ask about your personal icons. First of all, I hadn't realized Julia named you after the great Anna Magdalena Bach, nor that she was buried in a pauper's grave." Gertrude shook her head. "Then there is Philip Petit, who walked between the World Trade Towers in 1974. That was before you were born. How do you relate to that?"

"Petit lives near Woodstock and was Stevie's neighbor for a while. We hid in the woods several times to watch Petit practice walking between his two barns. We even took a bus to the city and lay on benches beneath the towers to concentrate on the space where he walked."

"So it symbolizes doing the impossible?"

"More like Petit showed us how to perform the imagined," Maggie said.

"Well!" Gertrude said. "I think I can say this without sounding condescending…"

Maggie nodded encouragingly.

"Your wobble between innocence and experience is so refreshing."

Maggie blushed. "Okay. I have a question for you. Do you have a few more minutes?"

"I've got to leave here in eight minutes."

"So, this research has led me to ask one essential question:

What's the best way for women to circumvent their lot in life? 1) Take a male name like George Eliot in order to succeed? In other words, slip through the cracks wherever you find them; 2) Or demand justice and accept the consequences like Rosa Parks; 3) Or follow your passion and take the calculated risk that the world may ignore your work?"

"Each takes immense courage. I suppose it's a matter of what you'd like to accomplish."

Maggie smiled and slumped on an elbow. "I know I'm not conventional. All I know so far is that being myself is the only way I'm confident. This doesn't rule out performing and putting on costumes. In fact, somehow, performance helps me express the issues I'm passionate about."

Gertrude nodded. "Did the research depress or stress you out?"

"No. It emboldened me."

"There is hope," Gertrude said. "There's evidence in Kenya that making safe houses for girls running away from FGM and giving them a college education is forcing the elders to rethink the practice. The graduates are building wells and schools in their villages and homes for their mothers."

Gertrude turned to the plate glass window, watching pedestrians pass on the sidewalk. It was Maggie who broke the moment of silence. "I'd like to raise a feminist son like Rip one day. How did you do it?"

Gertrude's face took on a new light mood. She swayed back and forth, smiling. "With love. And luck," she said. "But don't forget Gerrit gets credit, too. He was around for the first four years."

"I found the book you edited and read his article from the Vietnam War about the Napalm Girl. It was written so tenderly. His words clothed her with dignity."

"How did your mother raise you?" Gertrude asked.

Maggie hesitated. "There was a lot of joy at Old Red where I lived until I was twelve. I was lucky to have so many smart, caring adults around me growing up. Later we moved to town, and Julia paid me to nanny the twins. I suppose, traditionally, older sisters did this without pay." Maggie shrugged. "My childhood was short, but I was hungry for experience, and Julia always gave me the freedom I craved."

Sipping the last of her coffee, Gertrude looked at her watch. "Will you join us for Thanksgiving, Maggie? It would make us all very happy."

TWENTY-EIGHT

LEFTY GREW up in the Catskills and wanted his ashes tossed into the confluence of streams at Old Red. Arthur's partner, Kate, sang, and her sister played harmonica and guitar. Someone else played bongos. Joints were passed as Stevie stood on his tailgate, hawking Lefty's stuff for free—tools, clothes, furniture, and books. Maggie took one of Lefty's worn flannel shirts and put it on over her jean jacket.

"I'm staying with Agnus tonight," Maggie said to Stevie. "How about you?"

"Agnus will love that. Her place is beautiful. I'm going to Fern's."

"I have something for you," Maggie said. She opened her backpack and handed Stevie a small brown paper package. It was the triptych she painted—three small square portraits hinged together, enabling it to stand on a table. He admired her screws and hinges before turning it over to see the images: Lefty winked in the center; on the left, Stevie waved, his palm open and fingers spread; Agnus smiled blissfully on the right, eyes closed and arms folded over her chest.

"Thanks, Maggie." He kissed her cheek. He'd never done that before. So she kissed his cheek, too.

The first snow of the season fell as the light waned and the small crowd gathered streamside. Not wanting his father's ashes flying into the air, Stevie bent close as he poured them into the fast-flowing water. Everyone gathered for a full-body group hug. Maggie was concerned because she didn't see Arthur. She found him sitting in his studio with a plate of beans and rice on his lap. His hair was longer than usual; a knit cap pulled down to his bushy eyebrows. Lefty's passing had aged him. She pulled up a chair. They studied his new drawing of the owl and its magnificent wingspan. "I'm glad you made it to Beth's bird sanctuary."

Arthur nodded. "Beth and the owl were very patient with me. I drew for three days and then drove her way the hell off Route 28 somewhere to release him."

Maggie moved closer to his drawing: "It's how I want to remember him—flying." Already framed. Arthur's thousands of minute pencil lines were the same for the sky as the owl, which camouflaged him as he lifted off a pine branch. "Let me know how much when you get a chance. Don't let anyone else buy it."

"Take it," he said to her.

"No, I want to buy it. I can pay on time."

Maggie found Kate wiping down the kitchen counters. "Hey, that was a sweet send-off for Lefty."

"It's sad," Kate said, squeezing water out of the sponge. "I miss him. He was a brother to me."

Maggie pushed up her sleeves and stuck her hands in the warm, soapy water of pots and pans. Kate removed her apron and tied it around Maggie. "I told Arthur I want to buy his owl drawing. Please make sure he sends me the price."

Maggie was exhausted when she reached Agnus' two-bedroom bungalow. It was sparsely furnished and clean, with white-painted floors and walls. Before settling with a cup of tea and a blanket on the living room couch, Maggie washed her tear-stained face in the bathroom and removed the sad-looking painted buttercups, too worn to save. She slipped into a pair of sweatpants and a hand-me-down Angora sweater from one of the dancers and pulled the rubber band from her hair.

"Tell me your story, Agnus," Maggie said after a quick rundown of her own activities.

Agnus was also ready for bed. She wore flannel pajamas and wool socks. "My story doesn't make sense. Every word is a placeholder. How did I fuck up so badly? Where did all the years go? Did I really leave my six-year-old son only to return too late?"

"You arrived in the nick of time! You brought Lefty a lot of comfort. And you saved Stevie," Maggie said. Then she remembered a game they used to play at Old Red—"Give me one true sentence."

"Okay." She took a moment. "I'm very glad I'm back in Woodstock. My son is giving me a second chance."

"Yep. I'll tell you my true sentence," Maggie said. "You and Julia are good friends ever since living together at Old Red. It's too crazy that your paths have crossed, and now, once again, you don't live in the same town!"

"It's *bashert*, to use a Hebrew word. I came back because she begged me to. As it happened, she had little choice but to move with the twins' pretty-good father in California."

"Pretty good?" Maggie was surprised. "Because he sold the house out from under her?"

Agnus shrugged. "So here I am. Glad to help Stevie sort out his father's paperwork. Glad to give him a home. Glad to cook for him and to hike together. And I've gotten involved in some upcoming Byrdcliffe performances again as if I never left."

Rip picked Maggie up at noon. Gertrude made it clear that

Maggie and Rip were guests—they weren't to help in the kitchen —so instead of heading directly to the Thanksgiving festivities in Rhinebeck, they meandered into the Catskills. The tiny green Triumph, in need of a new muffler, putted up the winding mountain roads. He entertained Maggie with his professor's lecture on Chaucer's *Canterbury Tales*.

"Thirty-two pilgrims set out from the Tabard Inn to heal their sins. Each agreed to tell a tale, and the innkeeper promised a free meal to the best storyteller upon their return." Rip smiled and launched into the opening lines:

Whan that April with his shores soote
The droghte of March hath perced to the roote
And bathed every veyne in swich licour
Of which vertu engendred is the flour;
Whan Zephirus eek with his sweet breath
Inspired hath in every holt and heeth
The tendre croppes, and the yonge sonne
hath in the ram his halfe cours yronne,
and smale foweles maken melodye
That slepen al the nyght with open ye
So priketh hem nature in hir corages
Thanne longen folk to goon on pilgrimages

She clapped: "Who won?"

"The Wife of Bath."

"I have to read it," Maggie said. "Now, give me a story of your own."

Rip cleared his throat. "Krish is soft-spoken. Perfumed. From India. His father is in the textile industry. He studies business and is engaged to a woman chosen by his parents. But he falls in love with Linda from Chicago, and in the middle of the night, very quietly so as to not wake me, they make passionate love in the single bed three feet from me. And I can't help but come every time. This is how I survive without you."

"Well," Maggie smiled.

Rip grinned back at her. "Your turn."

She took a breath. "Okay, Tili. She's one of Ginger's dancers who shows up at the studio five days a week. She's a single mom from Rochester who pole dances in a downtown 'gentleman's' club to pay her rent. She boxes at an uptown women's club to rid herself of anger and to defend herself if need be. And she competes in triathlons to strengthen her muscles—which entails swimming across the East River and biking and running in all five boroughs. Out of necessity, she sometimes brings her beautiful baby daughter to Ginger's studio, who sleeps and wakes and never peeps."

Rip's eyes momentarily looked over his brow at her and insisted: "Another."

Maggie leaned back in the seat and closed her eyes. "Twice a day, my new love stares at me, and I at him. Twice a day, fresh water flows from Lake Tear-of-the-Cloud to the sea. Twice a day, the moon pulls the sea upstream. It's during this froth of salt and fresh that the riptide grabs me like the power of a train engine pulling into the station. Riptide is when I miss you most, sleeping in my little bed alongside the great gray river."

He grinned into the windshield. "I need to look at a tide chart."

"Turn right at the next driveway," she said.

As the Triumph circled onto the gravel, her hand settled on the back of Rip's neck. They gazed at the dark stone building of the Zen Monastery. No one stirred. "This is where Stevie practices zazen. I'm guessing it's where the Overlook stranger lives. Stevie says he knows my father." She pouted. "When I asked his name, he said he wouldn't say until it's safe."

"Safe?"

"I'm punished, and I've done nothing wrong."

"But your love might be palpable; you might accidentally betray him."

She shrugged. "We better get out of here. Let's go through Phoenicia and up the back way to Hunter. Stay straight along the Esopus, and we'll turn right before the next bridge."

Near the top of the pass, a small lake was visible through the woods. Maggie leaned against Rip to take in the view, and he pulled over at the side of the road. "This is where Stevie and I used to sail our homemade wooden boats. Sometimes they got caught in the middle when it was time to go, and we had to leave them or wade in and risk getting sucked by leeches."

Coasting down through a notch between mountains, the hamlet on the other side had a Western feel. A row of wood frame buildings with awnings over wooden sidewalks, all closed for the holiday. Maggie wanted to drive up the ski area to show Rip the view—the place the twins once played their fiddles with the Sizzling Strings. But the private road was closed, too, and they headed back down the winding road into the Hudson Valley. By the time they crossed the river and arrived in Rhinebeck, six cars filled Rip's driveway. They made a U-turn and parked across the street.

As Rip reached for the car door, Maggie whispered. "Wait. I love the photograph you took of my secret friend and me. I'm thinking of hiking alone on my seventeenth birthday. Maybe now that I live in the city, he'll talk to me. That way, nobody breaks their vow. What do you think?"

Rip nodded. "Please know that I don't expect you to tell me the secret, if one day you find out. But I'll share in your happiness, almost as if my own father lived again."

Blotting her watery eyes with a tissue so as not to ruin the yellow roses painted across her cheeks, she nodded. "Then I'll pursue my father for both of us."

TWENTY-NINE

TILI, her sister Nan, and baby Ada lived in a rent-controlled apartment in Inwood with the elevated number one train screeching to a stop every fifteen minutes right outside their fifth-floor bedroom windows. At street level, a tire store whined with its electric tools during daylight hours. Latin dance music from the next block boomed at night. The entrance to Tili's apartment building smelled like car grease, and the dust bunnies collected in the wide stairway. The apartment had two big bedrooms, a playpen in the living room, and a large eat-in kitchen.

Maggie got off the 1 train after the hour-long trek from downtown and accompanied Tili to the women's boxing club, a newly remodeled storefront space. Once the women stepped through the door, Maggie took a seat on a folding chair against the wall. She watched as Tili and her partner stepped onto the padded floor wearing helmets and gloves. They took turns practicing offense and defense. One managed exacting footwork as she threw fierce punches, jabs, and hooks while the other bobbed, weaved, and ducked, her feet hopping. Maggie felt pathetically weak as she watched. She had no strength in her arms, no metal in her fists. She never learned to throw a ball and couldn't remember ever hitting anyone. These women were warriors prepared to defend themselves.

"Let's go to a museum together," Maggie said when practice ended. "Which museum is your favorite?"

"I've only been to the Museum of Natural History," said Tili.

"Then we'll visit all the others," she said.

The following Sunday, just south of the big fountain in Central Park, at the plaza in front of the band shell, Ginger's company performed barefoot on a portable dance floor. The dancers looked like part of the fauna growing among the trees, with their sheer moss-colored capes draping their flesh-colored leotards. Yellow maple leaves drifted through the cool air. Their rhythmic clicking sound of rocks riveted the audience, too, even as a continuous stream of bicyclists and pedestrians passed in the background.

The outdoor performance fired up Ginger. Decades before, her company danced on the old piers that lined the Hudson River and atop the closed-down Westside Highway. Old friends and colleagues from back then joined the audience, clapping. They congratulated her and took her out afterward to celebrate. A flurry of dancers called in the following weeks to set up audition appointments.

"You won't be going home for Christmas?" Ginger asked Maggie.

"I might go to Carol's family Christmas Eve, but New York feels like home to me right now. Julia and the twins are planning a visit in the spring, and I'm saving to take a drawing class at The Art Student League."

"Years ago, I performed at the Maverick Theater in Woodstock with Carolyn Brown, John Cage, and Merce Cunningham. And I used to adore sleeping outside in the

Catskills. The Trailways bus dropped me off at Big Indian on Route 28, and I hiked into the mountains."

"By yourself?"

Ginger laughed. "I laid down my tarp and sleeping bag right out in the open. If animals licked my face in the night, that was fine with me."

"You have family in California?"

"My cousins and their kids. I need to see the Pacific every few years, or I get depressed. I'll be gone in a week. What about your boyfriend?"

"He's flying to Santiago with his parents to visit an elderly aunt."

A cold December descended upon the city and seeped right through the large industrial windows of the Westbeth loft. Maggie grabbed a sweatshirt and wool socks to wear and warmed herself by the oven as a potato casserole baked. As usual, she and Ginger enjoyed their cozy dinners at the kitchen table.

"How long has Tili been dancing with you?" she asked.

"A decade, I think. She was just divorcing and moved into an apartment with her sister in Inwood. She's very talented."

"So strong. I watched her box at the women's club. And baby Ada is so beautiful. Tili is such an attentive mother."

"The pregnancy was tough on her. She has lots of health issues, but she wanted this baby more than her own life."

"What about you, Ginger? No dream of children?"

"Oh, I dreamed alright, but after three marriages, I gave that up."

While Ginger was in California, Spencer, on the second floor at Westbeth, lost one of his little dogs to cancer. He was bereft and refused to get out of bed. Maggie continued to walk his little dog, Comet and brought Spencer a bowl of oatmeal in the mornings and soup in the evenings. But on the third day, his loft smelled so bad she tied a scarf over her nose and mouth as she swept and scoured his kitchen and bathroom. The fourth morning, she ran a bath and gave him a bottle of shampoo and bar soap.

"Spencer," she said as she was leaving. "You've got a full tub of nice warm water to soak in. Come on now. Be sure to wash your hair, or I can't walk Comet anymore. I'm allergic to dirt. I mean it. Throw Comet in the bathwater after you're done. He needs it as bad as you."

Snow fell, and the cold turned bitter. Mountains of snow piled up in the streets. Big salt crystals were spread on scraped sidewalks, but walking was still treacherous. Oil tankers broke through the ice on the Hudson as they moved upriver toward Albany. Maggie didn't mind being alone, but she was freezing as the wind blew through the old industrial windows. She bought a down parka at the Burlington store she noticed while walking Comet and ended up only taking it off to go to bed. Spencer's mood brightened. He accepted Maggie's invitation to Christmas dinner and arrived dressed in a suit with a bottle of wine in his hand. Her roast chicken, mashed potatoes, carrots, and string beans warmed his spirits.

"I like your flower," Spencer said.

"It's a painting of a lotus flower," Maggie said. "I like picking flowers for occasions and taking them off when I go to sleep. Where are you from?"

"Brooklyn."

"What kind of art do you do? I mean, this is an artist building, so I assume you are an artist of some type."

"Once upon a time, I was a bohemian poet and read aloud in coffee shops. Ginger and I used to have a good time."

"Oh?" Maggie said.

"I was husband number three," he said.

She smiled. "I didn't know."

"Her company danced to my surreal epic poems."

He thoughtfully blew on each forkful of food before putting it in his mouth.

"What happened?" Maggie asked.

"We had a falling out over Maybell, one of her dancers. Ginger just about killed me. I would have let her, but she stopped short."

"You fell in love with Maybell?"

"I made a mess of myself. Me and Maybell ran off."

"Shit," Maggie said. "That must have hurt." She got up and cleared the plates. "Would you like a bowl of vanilla ice cream?"

He nodded.

"How did you end up living downstairs?"

"This is where we met. In 1970, when Westbeth was founded. Maybell and I only lasted a couple of months. My tail has been stuck between my legs ever since."

After scraping his ice cream bowl with his spoon, Spencer washed his hands and rolled the old upright piano onto the dance floor. Opening the lid, he dusted the keyboard and brushed his fingers across the keys. He played something lively, the notes distinct, fresh sounding. Maggie took a blanket off her bed, wrapped up in it like a mummy, and laid down on the wide window sill to listen and watch the flickering harbor lights. Spencer began to hum and talk under his breath as he played, but his words made no sense to her. His transformation from a sour old man to an artist inspired Maggie. She ached for more life, more imagination, more freedom. Letting go of all but one edge of the blanket, it draped, twirled, and slid across the floor. As Spencer's fingers sped up, Maggie leaped across the loft, folding and bending to Spencer's untamed song. Her movements became torrential, like the eerie electrical storms at Old Red, when boulders crashed down the steep Cascade Brook. Maggie didn't know what she unleashed. Would Ginger call it dance? Spencer was mystified. When he stopped playing, Maggie collapsed on the floor, frightened by her abandonment. And then she stood up, laughing.

The first week of January, Maggie popped into the Art Student League on 57th Street. The registrar was only a few years older than Maggie and dressed down, unadorned by makeup. Maggie explained her history of drawing with Arthur and her portrait exhibit at the Woodstock Library. She also mentioned her experience as a class monitor at the Woodstock School of Art.

"The Woodstock School of Art used to be the Art Student League's summer school," the registrar commented.

Maggie knew this. She nodded and pointed to a motto on the wall. "What does *Nulla Dies Sine Linea* mean?"

"*No Day Without a Line.* It's an ancient quote by the Greek painter Apelles." The phone rang, and the registrar picked it up. Maggie watched a young man pass in the hallway, his jeans falling off. A woman wearing a smock. A man lumbering with a cane. Finally, the registrar hung up. "Are you looking for a drawing or painting class?"

"A life drawing class," said Maggie.

"Are you familiar with the League's philosophy? Professionals and beginners study side by side. Everyone is welcome. Registration is open year-round and runs on a month-to-month basis. You can start immediately, but to continue in the same class, you must re-register before the 21st of every month."

"I need an evening class."

"Classes are twice a week for two and a half hours. One starts at 4:30, and the last starts at 7:00. Or we offer two and three full-day workshops each month to choose from." Her eyes moved to another student, a young man about their age, waiting against the wall in the hallway. The woman smiled at Maggie. "Take a catalog and give me a call when you decide what you want. You can start as soon as you register."

THIRTY

MAGGIE AND CAROL took the bus to Woodstock the last day of April. Walking the icy city sidewalks all winter had been brutal. It meant walking around huge pools of melted slush at street corners and slipping on frozen litter and dog poop, not at all like walking the snowy paths of Woodstock. They shared Carol's double bed at her parents' house, whispering late into the night about Tili's boxing and go-go dancing and Carol's boyfriend's fashion photography, his dressing and undressing her, angling her this way and that as he fixed her in his lens.

In the morning, Maggie rose before anyone woke and baked her grandmother's World War II chocolate cake recipe. It was a drizzly spring day, and from the kitchen window, the Millstream across the street could not be seen through the new leaves. She decided to borrow a rain jacket for her hike up Overlook. Rip was working on a deadline and couldn't make it to Woodstock mid-week for her birthday, but they had plans to meet in the city the following weekend.

"Do you think you'd like to try it?" Carol asked, inhaling the fragrance of cake in the air.

Maggie poured her a cup of coffee and added milk. "What?" she asked.

"What we were talking about last night. Dancing at the men's club," Carol said. "The tips must be good. It's like dancing in a bikini at the beach."

"I'll ask Tili about it," Maggie said. "We'd probably have to audition. How would we even learn without a pole?"

Carol laughed. "There's a pole at the Woodstock playground. Let's take a look after your hike."

Maggie walked into town, crossed Tinker Street, and up Rock City Road to the Glasco Turnpike intersection. She knocked on Agnus' door. Her seventeenth birthday felt momentous.

"Hello, Sweetheart!" Agnus said. "What a surprise!"

"How are you?" Maggie asked without stepping into the vestibule. "I was wondering if you could do me a favor and give me a lift to the Overlook trailhead."

"Sure. Let me get my keys."

Stevie suddenly appeared at the door, too. "I heard your voice. I thought I was dreaming. Happy birthday, sis," he said. "Your birthday party is still on, right?"

"Yep. See you tonight, Stevie."

"You're in your underwear, kiddo," Agnus said. "I'm running Maggie up to Overlook."

Agnus knew the steep road by heart, jerking the Subaru to the right, then left, pushing on the gas, stepping on the brake at the hairpin turns. Maggie held on until Agnus pulled into the parking lot.

"Thanks so much, Agnus," Maggie said. "This five-minute drive saved me forty minutes of hard uphill slogging on the slippery wet pavement."

"Did Stevie tell you he dropped out of college? He gave up after only one semester."

"Don't be disappointed. He'll find his way."

"I'm trying to stay positive," she said.

Maggie put her hand on Agnus. "Don't be so hard on yourself."

"I guess what I really need is a good cry. Living with Stevie at nineteen is a real challenge, especially now that we're both home all day. I'm not sure it's going to work out. Maybe we can take a walk sometime this weekend if you don't mind."

"Absolutely, Agnus. I'm here for you."

As Maggie turned toward the trailhead, the stranger came toward her up Ohayo Mountain Road from the opposite direction. She waved. When they came face to face, he bowed his head, and she bowed hers. "Did you walk all the way?" she asked.

"Ten miles from Mt. Tremper."

"Do you know Magic Meadow? We could picnic there instead of hiking to the top, just this one time. It's only five minutes back the way you came."

No cars passed as Maggie and the stranger walked down the hill and turned onto the path. She directed him to a large flat rock, which seemed the best place to sit in the dampness. It was the same rock Carol lit with her graffiti the night they all jumped through Stevie's ring of fire. Now, a deer nuzzled the grass across the field, and the stream at the bottom of the hill was flooded with rain and melting snow. Two small birds flew out of the treetops and chased a red-tailed hawk.

"I used to come here with Stevie and Carol late at night to watch the fireflies and perform magic tricks. Do you live at the monastery?" she asked.

"Yes." He hesitated. Then he continued in his measured way of talking, with spaces between each word. "I took vows at the Zen Arts Center in Brooklyn while I was in college. In 1979, I moved to Woodstock to help renovate the Zen Monastery, which opened in 1980."

"That was the year I was born. What vows did you take?"

He reached his backpack for a canister of water and a paper bag, which he held out to her. She retrieved a piece of dried mango. "I took vows of harmony, self-restraint, and non-violence."

Maggie nodded. "My friend Stevie studies zazen at the Monastery. I attended one of the introductory meditations with him last spring."

"I know Stevie. His father recently died."

"Stevie and I grew up together." She chewed the dried mango and fished out her water from her backpack. Sun lit the meadow. Steam rose from the grass. "What do you think happens when you die?"

"When someone we love dies, we say, *May he or she reach nirvana.*"

"How do you define nirvana?"

"It is the state to which all Buddhists aspire: *the cessation of desire and the end of suffering.*"

"So, how does a Buddhist celebrate birthdays?"

"We walk into nature, like you on your birthday. *Nature is in a continual state of birth and death. To observe nature is to celebrate.*"

Maggie unwrapped two slices of the unfrosted chocolate loaf cake she baked and placed them on paper napkins. As they bit into the cake, crumbs fell into the cracks of the rock. He tipped his water bottle to his lips to wash the cake down. Maggie did not allow the words she was thinking to reach her tongue but secretly celebrated. *This is my father! We have celebrated almost every birthday together for a dozen years. We have eaten fruit or cake together each time. He loves me and Julia. Last year he met Rip, and he's Stevie's friend!* Maggie stood, brushed the last crumbs off her lap, and leaned against the massive rock. The sprinkling had stopped. The spring sun was taking hold. They listened to the hiss of insects.

"Do you have any other questions?" he asked.

She stood facing him. "I would like to know your name."

"Hum-Hum."

"Hum-Hum," she whispered, sliding her arms through her backpack: "Thank you, Hum-Hum. Hum-Hum," she repeated. His name lilted in her mouth. Skipping across the field, swinging her arms, she turned back for a last look. His clothing blended into the landscape, but she saw his head turn as his keen eyes followed her back up the road.

THIRTY-ONE

MAGGIE WAS PLEASED with her drawing class at the Art Students League. Two dozen students attended class each week, although not always the same students, so the teacher repeated key lessons to make sure that students built their skills on a solid foundation. The live models changed weekly also—men, women, young and old. Maggie adopted the League's motto and drew daily, during dance warm-up or rehearsal. By the third month, she decided that capturing the dance was her real fascination. She switched to oil pastels, but her drawings reminded her of Ginger's magic marker pictures. Taking her notebook to the pier on the Hudson, she returned to pencil and experimented with marking a small line for everything that moved, but her work resembled Arthur's. She started again with only two curved lines touching at only one point. To Maggie's surprise, this created a narrative she wanted to explore. Experimentation felt good even when she didn't know where it would take her. She learned at the Art Student League that her miniature portrait painting days were over.

Rip took a hotel for two nights near Astor Place, and they met up at a bar on the Lower East Side at 9:00 p.m. for the first set of a sketch comedy group. Maggie laughed so hard, and watching Rip laugh made her laugh harder. The actors drank beer with the audience, and on cue, two or three stood to perform a scene. The first sketch took place in a subway car with three straphangers rocking back and forth in unison, dipping and swaying as they discussed what to eat for dinner. When the train came into the station, they practically fell over. In another scene, two actors pretended to lie on a bed, their heads on pillows, staring up at the ceiling. One poked the other, tapped an arm, stroked a thigh, and the other responded with a pat, a kiss, and finally, they passionately gobbled each other up. Each skit lasted lasted only five minutes. Much too quickly, the one-hour set was finished.

Walking down Park Avenue to their hotel, Rip paused on the sidewalk. "I think you've grown, Maggie!"

"I've been working out. And Ginger's been teaching me to walk, to lead with my forehead and front of thighs. I have to keep my back straight and let my spine hold my head up, not my neck. Let my pelvis carry my weight. Philippe Petit said in his book that walking is always a balancing act. Locomotion and breathing developed together. I was getting winded trying to keep up with the dancers, so Ginger stepped in." Maggie unzipped her coat, displaying her figure. "Or were you referring to my breasts?"

"Yes. All of you."

"It's your love bites that did this to me," she said.

Saturday morning, they didn't call room service until past noon. It felt like Paris again or their weeks in Rhinebeck. Or after Gertrude's fabulous Thanksgiving meal when they locked themselves in Rip's bedroom for twenty-four hours.

"After Fern's party, when I didn't hear from you, I paid Stevie five bucks to drive me to your house, and we parked across the street. Stevie said I was lovesick. That's when he named you Dracula."

Rip laughed. "Tell me about your birthday weekend at Carol's house."

After rambling on about the cake and the lovely dinner Joan made for twelve guests, she offered him this, looking directly into his face. "The best part of my birthday happened at Magic Meadow. I shared a slice of birthday cake with the stranger, and he asked if I had any questions, so I asked him his name." Maggie let out a muffled scream, and they held each other tight. She squeezed her eyes shut and let out a long moan. "Hummmm." That was all she said.

Late in the afternoon, she painted tiny wildflowers of orange and pink spiky petals with yellow centers and dressed in an outfit she remade from a dress given to her by one of the dancers —a short skirt and vest of white faux fur and white boots. Rip looked his usual handsome, preppy self. They ate at a nearby Middle Eastern restaurant and headed to *Madame Butterfly* at the Metropolitan Opera. Maggie was entranced by the young Geisha, who falls for an American naval officer, but she didn't catch much of the plot, except that the Geisha's husband left her and returned with a new lover; they stole her baby, and she committed suicide. For Maggie, the tragedy was cushioned by the lull of the music and the Geisha's artifice: her white painted face, black lacquered hair, layers of traditional robes, and her tiny little steps.

Sunday, Maggie and Rip rose by ten. They were quiet, almost pensive, as their time together ticked down. From a discussion of the opera, their conversation moved to Rip's travels with Gertrude and Roland to Santiago and his usual Christmas trips to Rome. So attentively did Rip entertain Maggie that she began to wonder if, at any moment, he would deliver news of a new girlfriend. Perhaps this was their last weekend together. How could their long-distance relationship last? She accompanied him to Grand Central Station, and with an hour and fifteen minutes before his train to Providence, they got a table at the Oyster Bar, a white tablecloth restaurant on a beautiful mezzanine overlooking the busy station floor. He ordered sandwiches and coffee. Here, in the public eye, it was easier for her to ask about topics they had avoided earlier.

"How are your roommates?" she smiled. "Still keeping you up?"

"No," he said. "Krish and Linda broke up."

"Too bad," Maggie said. "Are you dating?"

"Not anyone special."

Maggie nodded. "And architecture?"

"I like my classes. Drawing comes easy, but building models is really time-consuming. I'm at the studio until after midnight most nights."

"What's your model?"

"I've designed a house for you. I named it Meadow House." He pulled a cardboard tube from his bag. "I photocopied the drawings. Let me know what you think. You're my first client."

She pointed to the ceiling. "Does it have constellations?"

He laughed. "It's modest. Modern. Made of glass and concrete with an indoor courtyard and a separate studio. I think you'll like it." He cleared his throat and smiled. "So tell me about yourself, Maggie. Did you fall for a model at the Art Students League? You're famous for that, you know."

She shook her head. "Besides, I've got Ginger and the company, Spencer and his dog. And Carol—we meet at Washington Square Park regularly. And I've become friendly with one of the dancers, Tili, and her baby named Ada. I told you about Tili—the woman who fights like a dancer and dances like a boxer."

"I still have mileage points on Delta. Shall we plan another trip?"

Maggie brightened. "Japan? *Madam Butterfly* is the ultimate face painter."

"I hear that in the old district of Kyoto, you can see Geishas crossing streets on their way to work."

"But imagine the jetlag," Maggie said.

"How about a cabin in the Adirondacks? There's a little museum at Blue Mountain I think you'd like, honoring hermits, guides, and trappers who lived in the backwoods."

"Mmmm. And a hike to Lake Tear-of-the-Clouds?"

Rip glanced at the clock in the center of the floor and waved his credit card to catch the waiter's eye. His train was scheduled to depart in five minutes. He quickly kissed her, squeezed her hand, and ran down the stairs. She watched him weave his way through the scurrying travelers and disappear through a door.

Before getting up from the table, she called her mother. They had talked on Maggie's birthday, but that was mostly about Julia's second postponement of the family trip to Woodstock. She was excited about several gigs she had booked. John wanted to take Toby and the twins camping on the San Juan Islands in August, which is how he spent summers as a kid.

"Ma, I'll fly out to visit you," Maggie said. "It's easier. What about Labor Day weekend?"

"That'd be great. I'll send you a ticket."

Maggie heaved a sigh. The city seemed especially hectic as she walked four miles from 42nd Street to the village, listening to the city flow like a river past her. Reaching Washington Square Park, she flopped down on a bench and called Carol to see if she could meet up. The upshot of the weekend with Rip was Maggie's renewed desire for him—just when she thought it might be waning.

Carol picked up her phone. "I'm just finishing brunch with friends. Are you okay?"

"I need coffee. Can you meet me? I walked from Grand Central to Washington Square."

Carol looked up at her table of girlfriends and tossed in two twenties. "I've got to run, guys. See you in the fall at the new dorm." The four of them high-fived.

Side by side on their usual park bench, Carol enjoyed hearing about the sketch comedy club and wooed at the details of *Madam Butterfly*. Maggie continued on about Rip. "I assumed we'd naturally drift apart living at a distance. In fact, all weekend, I expected he would tell me about a steady girlfriend. I wasn't expecting another case of lovesickness. I swear, I'm his moon. His gravitational pull is so strong."

"Yeah, watch out. It's hormonal, Maggie," Carol said. "Remember? I got pregnant."

Maggie threw her hand at Carol. "When does it go away?"

"Don't wish that. Observe how many products there are out in the world to make women feel desired like that again."

Maggie sighed and changed the subject. "What's up with you?"

"I landed a double internship this fall with Young Playwrights and the Vineyard Theater, working with public school kids, writing and performing."

"Cool," Maggie said. She tossed her empty coffee cup into a garbage can. They laughed, noticing that they both happened to be dressed in matching black tank tops. Maggie's cheek rested on the small birthmark of Carol's shoulder. She remembered the time Carol had asked her to look at it under a magnifying glass and draw a picture. It was a tiny dragon. From thoughts of Carol's birth parents, she leaped to Hum-Hum. She quickly pressed her tongue against her front teeth the way Stevie taught her, to stop her from spilling the beans.

"I'm thinking of the Millstream's cool, wet fingers," Maggie said instead.

THIRTY-TWO

JULIA DROVE up to arrivals in a silver Prius and tooted at Maggie, leaning against a pole with her small backpack. It was the Friday of Labor Day weekend, and the San Francisco International Airport traffic was backed up. Maggie walked out between two rows of stopped cars and hopped in. She kissed her mother. Julia looked rested, her face freckled, and her hair lighter and longer, halfway down her back.

"No Mick and Mia?" Maggie asked, looking in the back seat.

"They're with friends. You'll see them at dinner."

"I can't wait to get my hands on them!"

"Toby is still with his mother until Tuesday, so you won't get to meet him."

"How's it working out with the three of them?"

"They're treating each other like siblings. Mia is the odd one out, but she's learning to stand up for herself."

"Are you happy with their school?"

"Yeah. The public school's great. The big difference here is that John is a Seventh-Day Adventist, so there is church on Saturday. He is not strict on all the rules—but at home, he prefers no dancing, caffeine, drugs, alcohol, tobacco, red meat, and no risqué clothes or fancy jewelry."

"Wow. Did you know about this? I mean, Ma! Do you go to church on Saturday?"

"No. But the kids go." Julia looked over at Maggie as they sat in traffic. "It's okay. John's a sweet man."

Maggie remembered Agnus calling him a *pretty good guy.* "Did you guys break up because of his religion back when?"

"No. He converted when he married his first wife. John left me because I had an affair with David—our next-door neighbor."

"Yuck, Ma! David grabbed my ass in the Millstream once, and I told him off."

"You never told me that!" Julia stole glances at Maggie.

"Ma, keep your eyes on the road. You're making me nervous."

The twins were going into second grade. Deeply tanned, with brown, honey-streaked hair, they had grown at least two inches over the last year. Mia, taller than Mick, wouldn't let go of Maggie's hand now that she had an ally. They shared the double bed in Mia's room, which Mia rejected at first because John had painted it pink and the boy's room blue. But Julia encouraged her to hang her drawings like a gallery, and she made peace with it. Maggie played on the swing set in the backyard with the twins, and when they were tired of that, they walked two blocks to show her their school. They played tetherball, which Maggie no longer let them win. She noted that the rope was strong and pole solid and went back in the middle of the night when she woke to John's snoring. Kicking off her sneakers, she shimmied up the pole and sat on top of the ball. Pushing off, she swung around and around. Then, standing on the ball, she gripped the pole with her hands and feet. Lowering her head, she hung upside down and grabbed the pole at the bottom like an insect.

As blood drained to her head, she awkwardly lowered one foot at a time to the ground, unlike Ginger's dancers. Tili once so elegantly sat on the floor with her legs out straight in front, and leaning into her right leg, she brought the other around behind into the splits.

"We saw orcas swimming," Mia said when Maggie asked about their vacation in the San Juan Islands. "And dug clams when they squirt up in the mud. That's how you know where to dig."

"What did you like, Mick?" Maggie asked.

"I steered the speedboat," he said, shyly smiling.

Mia tugged on Maggie's sleeve: "I steered the speedboat, too."

"I lit the bonfire," Mick added.

Mia butted in: "And we made s'mores."

Sunday morning, Julia packed food, swimsuits and towels, sunscreen, hats, and water. Maggie sat in the back seat of John's Jeep with the twins, and a couple of hours south, they stopped at the upscale town of Carmel, which had a beautiful crescent-shaped public beach. It was a happy place like the Woodstock Green, with so many friends and families strolling with dogs. Surfers in wetsuits paddled, waiting for a wave. Small houses with twisted pine were visible all along the shore. At the far end stood a small private golf course. On the other, a house with a stone wall jetted out into Carmel Bay.

"That's the Clinton Walker House, designed by Frank Lloyd Wright," said John. "His signature single-story house. Notice the horizontal windows and the triangular foundation like the prow of a ship. It has only one right angle. Totally private, yet it's wide open to the Pacific."

Maggie pulled Julia close to the edge of the lapping waves. "Ma, can you take a picture of me in front of the house? I want to send it to Rip."

Julia ushered Maggie into the foreground.

"I remember Rip," John said. "A terrific guy."

Maggie nodded. "He is studying architecture at Brown. Where did your interest in architecture come from?"

"It's a hobby."

"Mick and Mia," Julia called. The three of them nervously searched along the shore. Two children were easier to spot than one—and there they stood, like birds ankle-deep in the cold water, watching the surfers in their colorful wetsuits ride the waves. The twins couldn't take their eyes off them, even as Julia marched them onward, pulling them by their hands.

Driving farther south, they stopped at Point Lobos and ate ice cream cones as they watched mother sea lions swim with babies on their bellies. Back in the car, they continued on to Purple Beach at Big Sur. Paths took them along a swamp and a stream to the dunes. Beyond the breaking waves, a wall of blackish-purple stone stood like a castle, with squares and rectangles cut out of it like windows. Every fifth wave spilled white froth through the openings. John spread a large blanket over the purple sand. Julia set out cookies, water, cheese, and grapes on a log. The twins dug with shells, building roads and houses which they decorated with feathers and driftwood while Maggie and Julia opened paperbacks, and John rubbed his white skin with sunscreen and shut his eyes. Later, when John joined the twins digging in the sand, Maggie and Julia took a walk.

"I met the Overlook stranger at Magic Meadow this past birthday," Maggie said.

Julia stopped and listened. Mistrusting her own daughter, she refused to respond.

"I asked his name. Hum-Hum."

Julia's jaw clenched, but Maggie took her arm, urging her to continue walking, and swiftly changed the subject. "Agnus has a sweet house. She's upset that Stevie dropped out of school. There's tension with both of them living together full-time."

The breeze stiffened. Julia wrapped her arms around herself. Strands of damp salty hair stuck to her face. "That's too bad."

"I don't know if Agnus will stay in Woodstock," Maggie said. Julia nodded in agreement but refused to say more. They seemed to have hit upon yet another subject Julia didn't want to discuss. Maggie was startled and saddened that her mother harbored secrets, not just the one. Plural. She felt a space between them. Agnus, Ginger, Joan, and even Gertrude seemed emotionally available to Maggie. Why not her mother? Glancing out at the rough ocean waves, she wondered if Ginger knew of Purple Beach and decided to collect a bag of sand for her.

"How is the dance company working out?" Julia asked.

"I was just thinking about Ginger," Maggie said. "It's going well. We get along. I participate in the hour-long warmup five days a week. Dance is challenging. I enjoy drawing the dancers more. I took a live model class at the Art Student League, but at this point, I'm leaning toward abstraction."

"How old is Ginger?"

"Early seventies, I guess. She's energetic and keeps up with her dancers, but two weeks ago, she fell off the ladder climbing to her loft bed. As only a dancer could, she rolled backward across the floor and howled with laughter. She wasn't even hurt."

Recently, Maggie had begun tracking Ginger's habits. She wondered about her numerous doctor appointments and loss of appetite and noticed that Ginger no longer took second helpings. She spent nine hours in bed instead of eight. And sometimes up to forty-five minutes in the bathroom. Yet she was stoic and energetic five days a week, with rehearsals from 10:00 and 2:00. And Ginger had begun joining in the warm-ups, something she hadn't done since Maggie arrived.

"*Don't help me up, Ma-Gee,* she said. That's how she pronounces my name, like her own last name."

"That's endearing," Julia said.

"I fall alone, and I get up on my own. That's Ginger's rule. So I set a chair next to her to help pull herself up. I offered to switch beds so she wouldn't have to climb up the ladder anymore. Ginger was so happy. She said, *Would you do that for me? Really Ma-Gee? I would be so grateful.*"

"So?"

"Yeah. I brought her things down from the loft, changed the sheets, and tucked her in bed. The next day, she ordered a double bed—mine was a single—and I found theater curtains at the Salvation Army I had dry cleaned. The super attached metal curtain rods that hang from the ceiling giving her a larger, private corner. And she bought a TV. Spencer, her third husband, lives downstairs and promised to look in on her while I'm gone. He brings her *The New York Times* and ice cream, even though she claims now she's not supposed to eat it anymore."

"She's lucky to have you."

"So I moved my computer out into the studio next to the piano and painted the loft bed and hung some of my things on the walls up there. I have more privacy now, too. Before I left, I quizzed Ginger about all her doctor appointments, and she said, *I have massage appointments and therapist appointments, acupuncture for my aches and pains, and a podiatrist for my poor ballerina feet. Ballet is a form of torture. Girls are subjected to it unknowingly, and it should be banned worldwide. I always tell all my dancers to take special care of their feet.*"

THIRTY-THREE

RIP'S drawing of *Meadow House* now hung on the wall above Maggie's loft bed next to her small portrait of him. These calmed her after watching murder mysteries with Ginger, classics like Hitchcock's *Rear Window, Dial M for Murder,* and *Strangers on a Train*. In her dreams, she roamed in and out of Rip's house as the glass walls opened on both sides of the living room. She hoped to one day build it but couldn't see that far into the future. In the meantime, dreaming about the house helped her sleep.

Ginger poured the purple sand into a glass bowl and encouraged her dancers to run their hands through the strange-colored grains and let the sand sift through their fingers. *We have to practice using our senses to understand the sensuous world. We touch things to know them. Our fingers are like little radiators, allowing heat to leave our bodies. Like our arms and legs, the best dancers know how to lift them and let them fall, each like a different note on the piano. Let's start our warm-up exercises with our fingers. Think like an octopus. A bird's wings. Fish fins. Now lift and drop your wrist, spread your elbows, and rotate your shoulders.*

Ginger invited Spencer for Sunday dinner. Maggie made mushroom soup, seasoned rice, and salmon in a lemon sauce and picked a large bouquet of mini-sunflowers from the roof garden. Spencer played the piano, and after, the three of them held hands and danced across the floor following Ginger's lead as Spencer recited poetry. Maggie was invited to watch *Double Indemnity* with them but took the opportunity to slip out of the building for a brisk evening walk through lower Manhattan. Her hair bounced in the wind as she made a loop past the monuments of human failings: the Irish Famine Memorial in Battery Park; the Native American Museum in the old US Customs House at Bowling Green; the New York Women's Foundation for Justice; and under excavation near Chambers Street, the oldest African burial ground. Walking back down Bethune Street toward Westbeth, yellow leaves rattling in the wind beneath the streetlights reminded her of fall in the Catskills and the eagles soaring over the Ashokan Reservoir. Once she unlocked the Westbeth door, she called Stevie from the inner courtyard.

"I'm missing you," she said. "Where are you?"

"Drawing. In my room at Agnus' house."

"That sounds cozy."

"Not. My truck's in the shop. The radiator's shot. I'm stranded."

"Get on a bus tomorrow and come into the city."

"Can't. I'm working Monday through Friday at the hardware store."

"Are you seeing Fern?"

"On and off."

"Are the leaves turning?"

"Yep."

"Don't you miss me?"

"You and Carol are my best friends."

"Come down this weekend, and we'll hang out. Maybe we can sneak you into Carol's dorm room."

"That'd be fun. I'll let you know."

He didn't make it for a few weeks, but the plan was in place when he arrived. Stevie dressed as himself in jeans, a plaid flannel shirt, and a baseball cap, while Maggie and Carol bulked up in men's shirts, sweaters and jackets, hats, and baggie pants. Carol had cut her straight hair into a shag that hid her eyes and went up around her ears like sideburns. A fake mustache was glued over her lip. Maggie wore beat-up sneakers, jeans, and a t-shirt, and her bulky hair was tied under a wide-brimmed hat. Tili had fake IDs made for Maggie and Carol, which got them into the club on Murray Street where she danced on Saturday nights. The man at the door took their entrance fee without looking at them. Inside was dark and crowded. Stevie went to the bar and ordered a round of beer while Maggie and Carol sat as they had practiced, bent over the table, legs spread apart, talking in low voices without smiling, their eyes square on the cabaret-style dancers. Maggie immediately spotted Tili's muscular torso in the female lineup. All of Ginger's dancers were particularly strong, but Tili's body rippled. The second set involved a striptease with three dancers wiggling and shimmying their nearly bare skin.

"We could do better," Carol whispered.

Maggie became distracted by a man in a long black coat standing against a wall, his collar up around his neck like the man at James' poker table. She had to pull her eyes off him so as not to catch his attention. Later, she spotted him only two tables away, hatless, his eyes hidden beneath sunglasses, his chin blackened with a goatee. Signs posted said no photography allowed, but Maggie saw the flash of his camera several times. He seemed to be shooting Tili specifically. At the stroke of one, after Tili's spectacular solo, the three shuffled out as planned and kept silent until several blocks away from the venue. Then a whooping howl let loose. Pulling off their disguises, they stuffed them into a backpack. At Bethune, Maggie waved goodnight and headed West while Stevie and Carol continued north, wrapped arm in arm. Maggie giggled, thinking of them squeezed into the narrow dorm bed as she had many times with Carol.

Life beyond her fellowship with Ginger began to loom in front of Maggie. She fantasized about applying to the Rhode Island School of Design to be close to Rip for his senior year, but it was an expensive private school, and she doubted she could get a scholarship. Carol's hankering to squeeze all the last bits of fun out of New York, including auditioning at the men's club, distracted Maggie.

"Juliette," Rip said lovingly when she answered her phone one night. "I've accepted an offer to study in Europe with my professor in the spring semester. He's writing a book on Filippo Brunelleschi, an architect and sculptor born in the 14th century." That was really all she heard. The name Juliette paired with the word tragedy, which she immediately imagined unfolding before her eyes. Her choices included poison, drowning, and checking into a convent. Then her mother's words filled her head: *Love is never a tragedy.* Her ears buzzed with bees, and she bucked up.

"Rip, how exciting. It'll be your last semester."

"Promise you'll visit."

"I do," she said.

They both laughed the way those two loaded words slipped out of her mouth.

THIRTY-FOUR

TILI WAITED for Maggie beneath the dark gray concrete overhang of the Whitney Museum with her one-year-old daughter, Ada, asleep in her stroller. The air was dense, threatening to rain, but the two women had big, warm smiles for each other.

"This building looks like a prison," Tili said to Maggie in her lilting island accent.

"Sunlight destroys paintings, and fewer windows means more room for art," Maggie said as she stepped in line to purchase tickets. At the elevator, she asked Tili: "Do you want something to eat first or after?"

"Let's keep moving since Ada is asleep."

They started on the third floor, meandering past Joseph Stella's scary futuristic *Brooklyn Bridge* and Edward Hopper's *Early Sunday Morning*. Maggie followed at Tili's pace. She finally paused in front of Willem de Kooning's abstract portrait, *Woman and Bicycle*.

"What do you think?" Maggie asked.

Tili chuckled. "It looks like a bunch of toddlers made it."

"That's a compliment," Maggie said. "It's hard to be that

natural. I could see my twin siblings sitting on the floor with crayons and paint and markers."

"I didn't know your little siblings were twins," Tili said. She shivered in the air conditioning and pulled a sweater out of the bag hanging on the stroller. Ada arched her back, whimpering, and tried to get out. Tili unsnapped the shoulder straps and picked up her daughter. Maggie moved Tili's bag to the seat of the stroller to keep it from tipping and pushed it as they walked.

"The twins are nine years younger than me," said Maggie. "I nannied them while my mother worked. I guess it's what big sisters do. I miss them. They all live in California now."

Ada, still in her mother's arms, was entranced by all the faces of strangers at eye level. Suddenly, she wanted down and, not quite walking, gripped her mother's pant leg in her fist. Tili pulled the little girl along as she stepped toward a painting of a dark-skinned shirtless man in a monochrome background. The strong light on the left of the painting highlighted his nipples, his strong arms, and his facial features. After reading the placard, she turned to Maggie and sighed. "This is my type of guy. Rugged and strong. Oooh! It says he's a French-Canadian boxer!"

"You're looking to fall in love?" Maggie asked, pulling her on. "What do you think about this? It's called *Luna Park*, by Joseph Stella. From 1918. It's Coney Island."

"It reminds me of the chaos at the prison for girls I was sent to at sixteen. When the night house mother got drunk and forgot to lock our doors, all hell broke out. Sex. Fist fights. Kitchen raids."

"What do you mean?"

Tili kept walking. "When I was twelve, my mother gave me to the state. I hated the orphanage. At sixteen, a judge sent me up the river until I aged out."

"A prison?"

She nodded. "They called it a school, but we were locked in. I never told anyone, not even my husband."

"But it wasn't your fault. You weren't a criminal. You were a kid in need of a home."

Ada began to cry, and Tili strapped her back into the stroller and settled her with a bottle.

"Let's get something to eat."

"I have to use the facilities," Tili said.

"I'll wait out here with Ada," Maggie said. Pushing the stroller in circles, she tried to remember the twins at Ada's age. Living in the country, they didn't use strollers. There were always enough adults at Old Red to carry the little kids wherever they went.

"What are you doing with that baby?" a stranger hissed on his way to the men's room.

"What?" Maggie said, confused. At first, she thought he meant that she wasn't old enough to have a baby. Then she realized he was referring to Ada's amazingly silky dark skin and hers, almost as white as his. "What a pig," she said out loud to no one. She wanted to complain to a guard that there was a sick-o in the men's room, but what good would that do?

"I was getting worried about you," Maggie said when Tili finally reappeared.

"I'm sorry. My sister called. She's not feeling well. We've got to head home."

"No lunch?"

Tili shrugged. "Maybe just a quick cup of coffee."

The partially underground cafeteria had a large window with a garden view. Tili was reading Ada a book when Maggie set the tray with two coffees and a bowl of rice pudding on the table. As Tili stowed the book in her bag, Maggie asked, "When were you married?"

Tili smiled, wondering why Maggie wanted to know. "Only once for twenty-five years. That was enough."

"But you are only... how old?"

"Ada is my miracle baby," Tili said. "I got pregnant at forty-five."

"Really!" Maggie said. "You look decades younger." The man's slur echoed in her head as she began spooning pudding into the baby's open mouth. Leaning in, she said to Ada, "Are you the best baby in the whole world?"

"It's raining," Tili said, disappointed. "I'll have to take the 79th Street crosstown bus. Want to come with us and take the downtown A or C train?"

"No, I have an umbrella. I'm going to walk across the park. It's one of my happy places." Then she continued. "Your sister was in bed the two times I visited your apartment. Is she sick?"

"She has MS and can't get around very well anymore. She needs a wheelchair, but that's impossible living in a walk-up. My daughter is about to walk at the same moment my sister can no longer walk."

"And you are a dancer!" Maggie said. "And a boxer!"

"I live on my feet," Tili laughed. "By the way, is Carol up for our pop-up dance performance in Inwood on Saturday?"

Maggie nodded. "She is if the sun shines. I have costumes. But we still need a name."

"The Three Little Pigs?" Tili laughed. "The Three Stooges?"

"No, silly. How about The Shooting Stars?"

Tili shook her head. "Definitely not in my crazy neighborhood."

"How about the Starlights?" Maggie said, finishing her coffee. She took Ada's little hand and sang: "Star light, star bright, first star I see tonight; I wish I may I wish I might have the wish I wish tonight."

"Yeah, okay. Let's decide tomorrow."

"The Starlings could be nice," Maggie continued as they packed up to leave. "It rhymes with darlings. And starlings flock together like a dance, swaying this way then that."

They crossed Madison and hugged goodbye. "You're the first person I told about my incarceration, and you know what? I feel the shame and guilt beginning to slip away. Thank you, Maggie, for taking me to the museum."

"Because you're not guilty," Maggie said. "Looking at art helps us figure out who we are and what stories need telling."

"Is that it?"

The traffic light turned red, and the green walk sign lit up. They crossed together and waved, heading in opposite directions. Winding her way through Central Park from East 79th Street to West 72nd, Maggie felt like Nature herself, one with the grass and trees. Tili shouldered Ada, her sister, and the whole crazy world, yet she was an excellent mother, sister, and friend. She takes care of herself.

Maggie got off the train and walked over to Chinatown to shop for dinner: miso soup, spicy peanut soba noodles, sautéed mustard greens, and sea bass. Ginger's request for interesting dinners had become a reason for Maggie to explore neighborhoods. When she learned about Middle Eastern shops on Atlantic Avenue, she took the R train to Court Street and bought spicy, briny olives, feta cheese pastries filled with eggplant and peppers, chicken cooked with za'atar, chocolate halva and pistachio baklava.

"What will I do without you, Ma-Gee?" Ginger said one night. "Seriously. Maybe you should stay on. I can cancel my search for the next candidate."

"We're family, Ginger. I'll stop by once a week to make dinner for you and Spencer. And I won't forget the holidays."

"Where will you live?"

"Not sure yet. I'll find something."

Maggie didn't want to spend her hard-earned money on rent, yet she really didn't have a plan. She told Ginger about the first dance she and Tili and Carol performed in Inwood Park to scratchy Spanish music, describing Tili's fancy footwork and air punches, Carol's sexy teasing gestures on the swing set, and how she stuck to her daily studio warm-up. At the end, a rowdy crowd of locals tossed coins and dollar bills into a hat while Tili told exuberant stories in Spanish that made everyone laugh and clap.

The following weekend, a saxophonist and bongo drummer showed up, and the three dancers wheeled and twirled across the tennis court and swung from the poles of the old metal swing set. A photographer with a big black mustache and long hair set up a tripod behind the dancers, capturing the faces of both dancers and the audience. A bare-bellied man took a wad of gum from his mouth full of gold and pressed a twenty dollar bill to Carol's forehead. The crowd moved closer, yipping, whistling, and clapping, egging the dancers into smiles. And they each took home nearly seventy-five bucks.

Maggie made a coffee date with the photographer. His name was Saxton, and they met in the village. He got her number from Tili to discuss a job. She didn't recognize him at first, with his dark hair tucked behind his ears and his clean-shaven face.

"You look different from Saturday," she said to him. "Delicate. Almost beautiful."

He shrugged: "I like costumes."

"I remember you at the Gentleman's Club six months ago taking photographs of Tili dancing," she said.

"I didn't see you."

She snickered. "I was dressed as a man."

"Oh, I thought you meant you were dancing."

"I went there to see Tili." Maggie sat up tall and gasped. "Shit! You are Dylan's Man in the Long Black Coat at Lew Beach!

With every meet-up, you look completely different. Why didn't you tell me? Did you get your movie made?"

"I'm waiting for you," he said. Pushing their empty coffee cups to the side of the table, he brought out a stack of eight-by-ten color photographs. She paused at the shots of the dancers' asses juxtaposed with the looming man with the golden teeth, his gross red tongue hanging out. They reminded Maggie of the Fellini movies she watched with Rip, circus scenes she didn't believe really existed.

"Have you been stalking me?" Maggie asked.

"I'm a filmmaker, art dealer, graffiti artist, entrepreneur," he said. "I take my entertainment work seriously, but I also enjoy myself. I like to make other people happy. That's when magic happens. I've been looking for the right partner for a long time, and I think we'd make a good team. I always do my homework."

"So, what do you know about me?"

"Through my mother, Lulu, I know Charlie Kim. I've seen your portraits on his wall. You do fucking great things with face paint. You're a self-made artist and performer. You're with the MaGee Dance Company. You're from Woodstock, home to the greatest Love & Peace concert ever." He paused and began to whisper. "I've got an idea how we could make five thousand a night in cash. We'll split it fifty-fifty. Say you perform once a week. That's ten thousand a month for four days of work. It entails a Saturday afternoon photo shoot and a late-night party. That's the commitment I'm looking for."

"Wait a second. Back up. Tell me about you."

"There's nothing to say."

"Well. Where'd you grow up?"

"New York City."

"Did you go to college?"

"I studied acting at the Strasberg Institute on 15th Street and later, Shakespeare in London."

"What's your favorite?"

"Shakespeare's love song to his son Hamnet, who died at age eleven. I've got many favorite sonnets. They're tongue twisters. Little mysteries, like the kind I thrived on as a kid. He pulled his hat down over his brow and made a snickery face.

> *To sit in solemn silence in a dull, dark dock,*
> *In a pestilential prison, with a life-long lock,*
> *Awaiting the sensation of a short, sharp, shock,*
> *From a cheap and chippy chopper on a big black block!*

Then Saxton stood tall, deepened his voice, and recited part of a sonnet:

> *The sea, all water, yet receives rain still,*
> *and in abundance addeth to his store;*
> *So thou being rich in will add to thy will*
> *one will of mine, to make thy large will more.*
> *Let no unkind, no fair beseechers kill;*
> *think all but one, and me in that one will.*

Maggie clapped. So did several diners at nearby tables as Saxton wiped his spit from his lips. When it looked like he was going to start again, Maggie pulled him down to his chair.

He leaned in for her to shake his hand. "Partners?"

"I need a place to live, preferably downtown, by the end of the month."

"I have a house in Brooklyn."

Maggie didn't respond.

"I'll see what I can do," he said. "Keep the photographs. Maybe they'll inspire you. And let me know when you're ready to start training for the film. I imagine you'll need to swim 365 miles, a mile a day, to prepare."

"I highly recommend Tili for the part. Her body is made of steel. As I recall, the character *swims* her house to the safety of the mainland."

"Only to realize the mainland isn't safe either. By the way, Tili doesn't swim."

"Oh! I didn't know," Maggie said.

He held out his hand for her to shake. It wasn't marble like Rips, nor rough and calloused like Stevie's, but a bit ragged like her own. "Do we have a deal?"

"Let's talk next week," she said.

Ginger was out when she arrived back at Westbeth, probably upstairs at the roof garden with Spencer, so she climbed up to her loft bed and shut her eyes. Why do I trust Saxton? Tili knows him. Maybe not well, but I trust Gertrude, and she and Saxton's mother are friends. And James somehow knows him. How bizarre. Finally, she picked up her phone and called Tili.

"Yep, his word is good," she said. "His mother collects women painters. He grew up in the city. He never keeps a lover for long, so watch that department, but I've not heard a complaint against him. Good for you if he wants to work with you, Maggie."

Maggie heard baby Ada crying in the background. "By the way," she said, "Saxton said you don't swim."

"I don't. But I want Ada to learn."

"I can make that happen," Maggie said. "I bet the 14th Street YMCA has swim lessons for toddlers. I'll take her."

"Oh, hey!"

"One last thing. What do you say when somebody on the street insults you? Shut the fuck up?"

"Say *that's racist*. Or *that's sexist*. Say it loud with the confidence of a school teacher so everyone within earshot gets educated. I've had to practice this long and hard because I don't want to accidentally kill anyone."

THIRTY-FIVE

IN THE MIDDLE of brushing her teeth, Maggie's phone rang. It was Agnus, her voice shaky. "Maggie…Stevie was in a car crash on Glasco last night, just down the road from my house. He must have been on his way home. I'm sorry. I can't think straight. I've put off calling you all day."

"What?" Maggie whispered. "How is he?"

"He flew out of the backseat of a car and hit a tree. He was pronounced dead at the scene. They say he broke his neck." Agnus began sobbing.

"Who was driving the car?" Maggie demanded. "Who was he with?"

"I don't know either of them. They aren't from Woodstock. The driver was under the influence. He was arrested."

"No!!!!!!" Maggie cried. She tossed her phone into the bathroom sink. Ginger came running.

"Darling, what's wrong?"

She sat Maggie down on her bed. Maggie knotted her hair in her fists as she sobbed. "My friend Stevie was killed in a car crash. Why wasn't he driving his truck? And why wasn't he wearing his seatbelt? Stevie always wears a seatbelt. It doesn't make sense."

Maggie caught a 6:00 a.m. bus to Kingston at 42nd Street. She was numb, her eyes swollen shut. Every so often, she wretched a liquid into a plastic shopping bag and wiped her mouth on the sleeve of her jean jacket. The woman sitting across the aisle from her moved to the back of the bus. She had called her mother twice and only got voicemail. Now, she couldn't stop herself from trying again. It was five in the morning in California.

"Ma," she said when Julia picked up.

Julia got out of bed and tip-toed into the living room.

"Ma, Stevie's dead."

"Agnus called me." Julia began to sob.

"I'm so sorry," Maggie continued. "I need you to come to New York. I can't do this by myself. I never thought I would need to ask you for something like this. I'm embarrassed. I just don't know how to go on without Stevie. Nothing makes sense."

"I'm coming, Maggie. I'll try to get a flight out this afternoon. Where are you now?"

"On the bus," she said, quivering. "Almost to Kingston. Thanks, Ma."

Maggie washed her face at the bus station while waiting to transfer to the Woodstock bus. The fresh air on her skin helped her breathe. She hoped Stevie thought of her kneeling at his side in his last moments. Getting off the bus at the village green, she walked up Rock City Road, past the cemetery and the baseball field, places she and Stevie knew intimately. At the intersection with Glasco, both sides of the road near Agnus' house were already filled with parked cars. Maggie wasn't prepared for that dose of reality. She turned in the opposite direction and searched for skid marks, broken glass, damaged foliage, police tape, anything to mark the spot. She threw up again at the side of the road.

The old two-lane Glasco Turnpike rose and wound around the lower slope of Overlook Mountain. A lone sycamore grew near the road on a small hill, its trunk white and limbs opening wide to the sky. She saw ten feet of mowed-down bushes on the north side of the road, and a tire mark creased the ditch. Maggie searched the tree bark for any sign of Stevie but found none. Opening her backpack, she tore the pages she wrote on the bus out of her journal and buried them in the loamy soil deep between its large roots.

Maggie let herself in the back door of Agnus' house and went straight to Stevie's room. After pushing the lock on the door, she climbed into his bed and cried herself to sleep. Not knowing how much later, she was roused by voices outside the window and then by a knock at his door. Still, she didn't move. Agnus finally used a bobby pin to pick the lock and noisily set a cup of tea on the bedside table.

"I'm sorry, Agnus. I should be comforting you."

"You are. You're here."

"Is Julia here yet?"

"No. But there is someone who would like to see you. The man Stevie studied meditation with. I don't think he is planning to stay long. You should make an effort to greet him."

Maggie sat up, pulled her feet to the floor, and looked at Agnus. A knowing smile crossed both their faces. Maggie pulled her hair into a rubber band and wiped her eyes. "You can send him in. But guard the door, please."

Hum-Hum stood in front of her when she opened her eyes. For the first time, father and daughter hugged. Her face pressed against his chest, she sobbed into his shirt, smelling of wood smoke, earth, jasmine, and salt. He felt good. Warm. Loving. They remained that way, not looking at each other but holding each other close.

"May Stevie reach Nirvana," Hum-Hum said.

Maggie whispered, "Death is the cessation of desire and the end of suffering. Nature is in a continual state of birth and death."

"When we meet at Overlook, we'll celebrate Stevie," he said. Then he stepped back.

"I'm sorry I missed you on my birthday," Maggie said. "Please forgive me. I've been caught up in... I don't know what."

Hum-Hum nodded. "It's difficult to find nature in the city, but the rivers and harbor, the parks can all give comfort." He bowed and turned.

She wanted to offer to drive him back to the monastery in Stevie's truck but quickly realized the danger it might cause if anyone noticed their burgeoning father-daughter relationship. He slipped out of the bedroom door, and moments later, she noticed him smiling at her from outside Stevie's window. She smiled back. It was the same smile.

Maggie changed into Stevie's red flannel shirt and a pair of his jeans. After washing her face, she joined the mourners. Kate and Arthur. Miriam and her husband and other people Maggie hadn't seen since she was little. She hugged Fern and friends of Stevie's she didn't know. The owners of the hardware store whispered their condolences. Carol and her parents had not yet arrived. And then she saw James.

Maggie hugged her. "I didn't know you knew Stevie."

"I came for you," James said. "We've got to comfort the living."

"I so loved riding Belle. How are they, Belle and Blackjack?"

"Fine."

"I have a question." Maggie pulled James over to two of the wooden chairs lining the living room wall. "The man in the long black coat who flew in to play poker. I met up with him a couple of times in the city. His name is Saxton."

She nodded. "A damn good poker player. He won big time that night, which is the reason you got a mere hundred bucks from me."

"He wants me to partner with him on a project," Maggie said.

"He's a chameleon, in the best sense. I've never known anyone quite like him. He has incredible creative energy."

"Like a red ball burning inside him?"

James shook her head, not knowing what Maggie meant, and continued. "My aunt lived in Saxton's mother's building on Central Park West, so I met him years ago. Recently, we ran into each other at a poker game in Boston."

"Saxton saw my portraits hanging above Charlie Kim's piano. It's all very convoluted," Maggie said. She rolled her eyes, confused. If she was a project for the adults in her life, she wished they'd give her a heads up.

Agnus called the morgue and requested some time alone with Stevie. She and Maggie were given a half hour. He was covered in a white sheet to his chin. His face shaved, his hair parted and combed, something he never did. Agnus had refused an autopsy and embalming. Like Lefty, Stevie would be cremated and his ashes tossed in the confluence of the Beaverkill and the Cascade. As they leaned over him, Maggie noted his bruised neck. Agnus saw it, too.

"Look at his beautiful long brown eyelashes…he had those as a baby," Agnus whispered, squeezing Maggie's hand. "How can I ever get enough of him? I missed so many years."

"Look how his lips turn up a little at each side of his mouth," Maggie said. "Like a wink. I think he's reached Nirvana."

The two of them had decided on the white Japanese anemone as his flower. Skipping the agar-agar, she set up her paints, mixing white with a dash of yellow, a dash of pink, and a dab of black. The side of her hand touched his cold cheek like a small electrical shock. She drew her hand away. Again, her hand rested on his cheek. This time, she left it there, feeling the chill. *I love you so much, Stevie,* she said aloud. Painting the six blossoms with six white round petals across his nose and cheeks, she remembered how it turned up when he was little and how, during middle school, a distinctive bump appeared on the bridge. *I will always love you, Stevie,* she said out loud, and then: *We never went camping with the twins!* She sighed. After painting the yellow centers of each flower, she kissed his forehead. Agnus took a long look and nodded when she was ready to go.

Walking back from the house, Agnus said, "You and I will go over to Old Red one day and put together a show of Stevie's sculpture."

Maggie agreed.

Back at the house, a haggard looking Julia had arrived, thanks to Kate and Arthur who picked her up from the Albany Airport. Mother and daughter fell into each other's arms and plopped down onto the couch with eyes closed, Maggie's head resting on her Julia's shoulder. It wasn't until dinner time, when Kate warmed food and set it out on the table, that the two of them let go of one another.

The following afternoon, Maggie drove Julia and Angus to Stevie's favorite haunts, starting with a drive-by of Magic Meadow. They got out only when they reached Byrdcliffe. Agnus walked them on the paths she knew so well.

"Lots of people lived here over the years," she said. "John Burroughs, Isadora Duncan, Dylan, Joanne Woodward. I lived in a cabin at the top for a few years before I knew Lefty. I missed Byrdcliffe when I left and came back to walk the paths when Stevie was a baby. Fall was always gorgeous."

Julia nodded. "I remember walking with you and Stevie."

At the Ashokan Reservoir, they strolled the causeway watching the bald eagles fish in the reflection of the Catskills.

Later, they slowed as they passed by Lefty's cabin, noting the tall grass his goats once mowed. Julia wanted to drive by John's house, which still stood empty, and the sight of the Millstream was like an old friend calling to them. They parked at the side of the road and dipped their feet into the water.

"Agnus," Maggie said. "Did Stevie know why you moved to California? Cause I've never understood what happened."

Julia squeezed Maggie's arm as if to hold her back. "I'll tell you one day."

"I can talk about it," Agnus said. "I developed a drug problem. I was always a pothead, and I liked cocaine. Oh, I dropped acid at the Woodstock festival like everyone else, but I had postpartum depression after Stevie was born, and I stopped nursing. I felt so guilty about it! Stevie was about nine months old when I tried heroin. The next thing I knew, I was addicted. I cared more about getting high than taking care of my baby. Julia got me into rehab, and I did okay until I relapsed. Lefty threw me out of the house. I wasn't a good mother."

"Agnus," Maggie said. "I'm so sorry."

"No, I'm the one who's sorry. Julia was the only friend who didn't give up on me. She got me into rehab again. This time in California, and it stuck. I've been clean for sixteen years, but I was always too scared to come back. Lefty had a new partner, and he was a great dad. Stevie wrote me a letter asking why I moved to California when he was twelve, and Lefty told him my sad story. I think it was about the time they moved to the goat farm."

"And Lefty introduced him to meditation," Maggie said. "Stevie was never into drugs."

Agnus nodded. "I'm happy about that."

"There was always a group of kids in high school who were high on something or other. Even in middle school," said Maggie.

Back at home, as Agnus was preparing dinner, Maggie told Agnus that she'd like to buy Stevie's truck.

"Take it," Agnus said.

"I promise I'll keep it running. I'd have to find a place to park it. And get insurance."

"We should transfer it to your name while you are here."

"Let's find out what it's worth so I can buy it."

After Maggie drove Julia to the Albany airport, she came back to Agnus' and collapsed. She slept through the night without dinner. Over coffee the next morning, Agnus scrounged around in a basket of mail on the kitchen counter and handed Maggie an envelope. She opened it and read:

Dear Agnus, I am writing because my wife and I are heartbroken to hear that your son, Stevie, died in a car crash on Glasco last week. I loved that boy from the time he moved with his father to my neighborhood. We'd meet at the mailboxes every so often, mostly in the summer. We had many beautiful conversations. He was curious, thoughtful, sensitive, and ambitious. Not too long ago, after his father died, he told me he brought his two friends to watch me practice walking the wire between my barns. Oh, I knew they were there. I got a kick out of my little audience laying on blankets in the woods, quiet as birds, but I didn't let on. Please know that you and Stevie are in our thoughts. I hope this brings you some comfort.

Philippe P.

THIRTY-SIX

"I JUST CAN'T STAND that he doesn't exist," said Carol. She and Maggie napped side-by-side in Stevie's bed. "That he is back where he was before he was born, wherever that is. I just hate it. I wish I never broke up with him. Maybe he'd still be alive."

"Come on, Carol," Maggie whispered to her friend. "Let's figure out something to do for Stevie. He always helped people out. Agnus said I could buy his truck. What if we got it tuned up, painted his name on it and a Japanese anemone, and donated it."

"To the Women's Center!" Carol exclaimed. "Women are always having to move from one place to another. It would really be a great help with picking up donations, too."

"Perfect," Maggie said. "We could offer to help write a grant to cover expenses. But you'll be in Europe next fall, Carol. Let's set up a meeting this week with the Women's Center."

The two friends fell back asleep and woke up energized. They outlined what had to be done to keep Stevie alive or at least his truck. After Carol left for the city, Maggie gave the notes to Agnus.

"I want in on it," Agnus said. I bet I could get twenty people to donate a hundred bucks, enough to hire an attorney to draw up a nonprofit agreement if that's what you want. Or enough to make repairs, paint it, get new tires or whatever."

Rip picked up Maggie on Saturday and drove her to Rhinebeck. Gertrude and Roland were there, and the four of them spent the afternoon in the shade of the walled garden where the bear and her cub once roamed. Sipping iced tea, they swaddled Maggie in their kind and gentle ways. It wasn't until dark, when they went in to cook dinner, that the conversation moved away from Stevie.

"I overheard Charlie Kim tell someone at a party recently that he is your biological father. Is that true, Maggie?" Gertrude asked.

"No," Maggie said, setting the silverware and plates down the table. "I mean, it's possible that he thinks it's true, but it's not. Charlie Kim is not the only man who claims me as his daughter. A handful of others have insisted the same thing to my face, but before Julia left for California, she told me that my father is dead."

Roland looked to Gertrude. "Oh, so sorry," she mumbled. "I shouldn't have brought it up."

"No," Maggie insisted. "It's okay."

As they sat down to a plate of pasta with garden pesto and tomato salad, Gertrude explained that her newly funded research grant included a survey of American memorials to women, state by state. Her students were enthusiastic about the project and signed up to research their home states. "I have a book contract due in January for the first phase of the project. You, along with my students, will receive acknowledgment for your help."

"Thanks," Maggie said. She had only eaten half of her plate of food when she took Rip's hand under the table. "I've had a wonderful day with all of you, but I'm afraid I'm fading. I'm going to have to leave soon."

"Why don't you sleep in my studio," Gertrude offered. "You were comfortable there, right?"

"Yes, very," Maggie smiled. She felt herself melting into the chair.

"Excellent idea," Roland chimed in. "No need to drive anywhere tonight."

She was half asleep when Rip came into her bed. "Let's run away to Morocco or Crete and swim and take walks, and you can design houses forever and ever."

"But our families aren't feuding," he said. "We don't have to run away."

"Oh, I'm so disappointed. You have a brilliant career ahead of you, and I have such an interesting life…but wouldn't it be glorious?"

THIRTY-SEVEN

WHEN THE BOSS' assistant whipped out a tape measure, Maggie stood tall. She held her forehead high, her pelvis supporting her spine. Tiny red tulips floated across her cheeks and nose. Breasts and hips were clad in a sparkly bikini that matched her skin tone. She had learned the simple cabaret routine in one hour.

"Hey, Flowers," said the assistant, "Get into line with the girls, the next set starts in five minutes."

Maggie nodded. Placed in the middle of the lineup of ten women, their flimsy costumes shined like one long, scaly dragon with a ridiculous number of high-heeled feet. Maggie was invigorated by the dance, and she felt she did well enough. Afterward, she was called over by the boss, Tommy.

"Where'd you learn to dance?" he said.

"Ginger MaGee's Company at Westbeth. I've danced five days a week for two years, and I've got a solo piece I'd love to show you."

"Give Flowers the one o'clock slot," Tommy said to his assistant.

Her dance was choreographed, yet she didn't recognize the

musical arrangement. She heard Ginger whispering—*free your body*—and Tili—*kick higher, taller*. Maggie relished having the stage to herself. Like the day Spencer played the piano, she felt the red ball burning inside, only this time it was controlled. Every now and then, she smiled at a stranger sitting at a table in the audience, pretending he was Stevie. She loved her own limber body. She pleased herself. Ginger would have approved.

"Let's give Flowers a hand," the boss yelled, stepping onto the stage. Maggie put her hands together, bowed, and walked off.

She hadn't mentioned her solo performances to Saxton. For more than a month, she danced several nights a week and made enough money to survive while she and Saxton got their act together. She told him her amended idea—not to paint news headlines like she originally thought but to graffiti her painted torso with a line of glow-in-the-dark poetry. She handed him a page of lines from her research, phrases of poetry that entwined body and language.

"I like the graffiti," Saxton said.

"For instance," Maggie read: *"Begin in the middle and end in the middle and it should all be there. V.S. Naipaul.* He, of course, was referring to writing, but it's sexy in this context."

He nodded, and she continued. "And I want a fully painted face, like a Geisha, only not white—a different pastel color every night. And a formidable wig, a big black beehive or something."

This time, he smiled. "I've got two exclusive parties booked. You'll be on my arm the whole time. No one will touch you. You open your coat, and you twirl on my finger like a ballerina. A video screen of you dancing plays on the wall all night long."

Saxton's photographs from the Inwood playground were instrumental in booking their first two parties, but he needed swank indoor footage to book higher-end subscribers. When Saxton's mother heard this, she called Saxton. "I'm having a dinner party on Saturday. Stop by with Maggie before your midnight gig. You can introduce her as Flowers and shoot some film."

He came dressed in tails and top hat, the whip coiled through his belt loop; Maggie had big black painted eyes, a mauve face, her hair a red architectural structure. The rest of her was hidden beneath a long faux fur coat.

"I'm Saxton's mother," Lulu said, introducing herself. "We met briefly at Gertrude's Hudson art opening. I've known her son, Rip, since he was born."

"Thank you for inviting me tonight," Maggie said.

"I was sorry I didn't make it to your Woodstock show. But I sent Charlie Kim in my place. How wonderful that he bought eighteen oil paintings! Kermit and I saw them the other day. They're little gems."

Kermit, her partner, took her hand. He was a gracious old master art dealer dressed in a three-piece suit. Maggie noticed his thick waves of reddish hair. "Your paintings of saints are like the Flemish painted in the 1400s."

"That's what I wanted to be as a kid."

"A painter?" Kermit asked.

"A saint. I painted everyone as saints."

Lulu looked at Maggie. "And you're also a dancer."

Maggie nodded. "A writer, a performer. For the last two years, I've been dancing at Ginger MaGee's studio at Westbeth."

Saxton moved through his mother's living room, entry, and library, lowering the music, adjusting lights, grouping his mother's guests, and setting up his tripod and movie camera. Lulu had Maggie on her arm so Saxton could set up the camera, and then he stepped in. Maggie curtseyed as the music began and danced, opening her coat partway for a few guests at a time. The words in gold graffiti across her royal blue torso read: *And your very flesh shall be a great poem. W. Whitman.* As always,

Saxton carried a small recorder in his pocket to capture sound ambiance and a camera around his neck to snap close-ups of Maggie and the guests.

"Please welcome—Flowers!" Saxton called.

With this new material, Saxton booked another batch of Saturday parties. He sold subscriptions to the life-size weekly photographs of Maggie's torso in black and white in order to reach a secondary audience. Charlie Kim was the first to subscribe. Next were his friends. And then friends of friends. Finally, the party bookings were stacked up three months in advance. When calls for out-of-town parties came in, Maggie put her foot down. She refused to travel for this gig. She didn't want to commit any more time to it.

"I'm glad you and Spencer have renewed your friendship," Maggie said one night to Ginger as they enjoyed chocolate ice cream. Ginger had rented *Kiss the Girls*, another murder movie, for the night's entertainment. "How are Spencer and Comet?"

Ginger grinned. "Spencer's nearly back to his old self. He and I had a great love early on, and it ended badly. Abruptly, actually, after only two years. It's the reason I don't allow men in the studio during rehearsal. I'm reluctant to give anyone a look at my dancers. Have you figured out your plans, Ma-Gee? I'm afraid to think of you on your own."

"But you managed alone in New York," Maggie said. "Saxton is vetted. I've met his mother, Lulu. I've been to her apartment on Central Park West, where Saxton grew up. We are working on a routine—a sixty-minute spin with him on my elbow through late-night party venues. It will pay my rent. I won't be homeless."

"What kind of dance?"

"It's a little cabaret, a genteel tease with a bit of literary graffiti painted on my torso. Quotes with a dash of humor. My name is Flowers. I'm not identifiable." She took a breath. "The

Woodstock librarian, Ms. James, introduced me to Saxton. He's hired a make-up artist to help me prepare."

"Give me an example of the graffiti," she insisted.

"Here's two by Emily Dickinson. *Bring me the sunset in a cup.* And *The lovely flowers make me regret I am not a bee.*

"Lovely, Ma-Gee," Ginger said. "But where are you going to live?"

"Still working on that."

THIRTY-EIGHT

MAGGIE TOOK a day job as manager of The Captain Kidd House on Pearl Street in the financial district, a tiny nonprofit that had been around since the 1950s. In what must have been their private library, she found a book about Captain Kidd's adventures written by his wife, Sarah Bradley Cox Oort, the wealthiest woman in New York City. According to her, Kidd wasn't the typical seventeenth-century pirate. He signed up as a privateer, along with many respected Englishmen, when the King of England wanted to plunder the Spanish ships trolling his waters. Kidd and his wife supported the building of Trinity Church, a few blocks away from their home, the place where she and their daughters are buried. Their social circle in New York included three governors, fur traders, explorers, and Robert Livingston, who had helped draft the Declaration of Independence, but none helped Kidd in his hour of need.

When Carol called to see how the job was going, Maggie told her about the twenty-minute play she wrote on the Kidd family. "It's geared to middle school kids who visit the House, so there's buried treasure, fencing lessons, and even a pillow fight. We hand out bags of booty that look like gold candy, but it's really candied carrots."

"I love it," Carol said.

"Maybe you want to sign up as a sub? Our educator, Jade, plays Mrs. Kidd, and she's got two daughters, Amanda and Zora, so we have a bunch of part-time actors. Jade deals with bookings and the students. I play Captain Kidd. I love walking around in a long black wig and mustache!"

"What do the students think about Kidd's spooky ending? Didn't the king hang him from the London Bridge?"

"It gets their attention," Maggie said. "That's when I dig in with my questions: *Is it okay to steal a ship? Or take over land that belongs to other people? Can you rely on rich or famous people to save your life? No? Then, whom do you rely on? Yes, Excellent! Yourself is the correct answer. You are responsible for your actions and for developing your character. Have you ever scapegoated anyone? Ever been used as a scapegoat? Can someone give me an example? What does it feel like?*"

"Put me on the sub list," Carol said.

"Oh, nice!" Maggie said. "Teachers sometimes sign up for a walking tour to Bowling Green Park, the traditional Lenape's trading ground. We discuss Peter Minuit buying Manhattan from them for a handful of beads. And that the neighborhood is still the center of trade with the stock exchange just around the corner."

Maggie didn't go into the fact that she was feeling pressured not only to find a place to live. The Executive Director who hired her, Joseph Jones, a British academic, was arriving in New York to attend the annual board meeting. Over the phone, she thought him exceedingly polite and smart and was looking forward to meeting him in person. It was the board members she wasn't so keen about. She had only been in touch by email with the man who did the website, but none of them had visited in the months she had been working there.

Maggie continued to spend Sunday nights in the loft bed at Westbeth. Her computer still sat on a desk next to the piano, and her books and clothes were stored in the loft. After cooking Sunday dinner, doing her laundry, and packing for the coming week, she'd pause at the industrial window to gaze out at the churning Hudson. When she couldn't sleep, she'd take a walk through the winding streets of Greenwich Village and call Rip. He'd tell her about his projects and his girlfriend Emilia, who was studying fashion at the Rhode Island School of Design. His words didn't matter as much as the sound of his kind, calm voice, which penetrated her soul. But sometimes, missing Rip triggered missing Stevie, even if the one never filled the other's shoes. And she mourned them as if they both had died.

"And you? And Saxton?"

"The same," Maggie said. "Saturday nights are working out. My bank account is growing. Saxton curates the whole thing— painting, dressing, and escorting me, as well as filming, photographing, recording, and editing. Sometimes, he feeds and shelters me. We share everything but the bed. In fact, I've been sleeping in Captain Kidd's bed Monday through Thursday–too bad he died centuries ago, as I am a little lonely. I often stay in Carol's dorm on Friday nights. I enjoy that little bit of college life. Saturdays, it's nearly dawn when we finish up with the performance, so I usually crash on some stranger's couch, wherever Saxton lands. Sunday, I'm here with Ginger, cooking dinner, watching some BBC murder mystery. I try to cook a few meals to leave in Ginger's fridge, and I still do her bookkeeping, so I catch up on that. Jones, my boss at The Kidd House, is flying in from England, so I'll finally have the pleasure of meeting him. His daughter plays Mrs. Kidd. She's terrific." Maggie paused. "Will you be in town anytime soon?"

"I'd love to see you. I'll look at my calendar and let you know."

When Mr. Jones and Maggie finally met, he asked her to call him Joe. They sat in the Kidd living room, sipping tea. She had removed the sheets covering the dainty old furniture, which were, of course, replicas, and placed a vase of roses on the side table. He was a small, elegant black man and wore a beautiful blue suit with a bow tie, a white shirt with suspenders, and highly polished shoes. Maggie had a class scheduled following their meeting, so she was dressed as Captain Kidd, minus the hat, the long black wig, and the curling mustache.

"The board, myself included, were tickled by the announcement in the educational section of *The New York Times* about the new program," he said. "Very flattering. Jade said all credit is yours. You wrote the play! Well, Well. And strolling through the House, I see that both toilets are in working order. The furniture and wooden floors are polished. And it doesn't smell moldy but aromatic!"

"I brew a sweet orange spice tea most evenings," she said.

"I haven't seen any mouse droppings, or mice, for that matter. The cat you took in from the shelter must be doing a good job. And the patio you excavated out back is brilliant, with seating for students and flower beds. The financials are in order. You passed the Board of Education inspection and a burgeoning partnership with the South Street Seaport Museum summer camp. Did I leave anything out?"

"What about sleeping four nights a week on the premises?"

"I don't mind. I spoke to most of the board members, and they acquiesced, saying that your presence is a deterrent to thieves. In the seventies and eighties, that was a problem. I apologize that I've been stretched so thin. Perhaps you'll win the board over, and they will step up to the plate. The meeting is next Thursday at 5:30. I'll send you the address. It's at the law office of Leonard Charney."

THIRTY-NINE

TWENTY-FOUR SEVENTH GRADERS were riveted on the back patio at the Captain Kidd House, watching the Kidd sisters fence, when Maggie's cell rang. It was Spencer. Ginger had fallen on the street.

"She didn't know what happened," Spencer said. "But a woman passing by helped her home. She had pieces of glass in her forehead and a black eye. I wiped up a lot of blood," Spencer said.

"I'll be there as soon as I can," Maggie said.

She let the head teacher know she had an emergency and that Jade would field the students' questions, but regrettably, the museum staff would not be able to lead a walking tour. She handed the teacher a flier with a map of the financial district and talking points, encouraging her to lead her students.

"Look what happened to my beautiful skin," Ginger groaned when Maggie arrived at Westbeth. She lay on top of the bed with a damp cloth over her left eye. In her other hand, she held a mirror, staring at her swollen cheek.

"What happened, Ginger," Maggie asked, sitting on the bed next to her.

"I don't know. I just woke up on the sidewalk."

"Did you call your doctor?"

"I called my naturopath and made an appointment for next week."

"We have to get you checked out," Maggie said. "But first, I'm going to make sure Spencer got all the glass out of your forehead."

Maggie put in a call to Lulu for advice. Sure enough, Lulu called her internist, Dr. Day, and got a noon appointment for Ginger. Maggie called Jade to ask if she could teach the programs at the Kidd House the following day and to find a sub to play the Captain. At Ginger's request, Maggie sent an email that tomorrow's dance rehearsal was canceled. Then she got Ginger into a cab. Lulu met them in the waiting room. Maggie expected a long ordeal, but Dr. Day's nurse ushered them right in. After a ten-minute consultation, Dr. Day insisted on ordering a full workup for Ginger.

All the while, Lulu couldn't take her eyes off Maggie. She was shocked to see her unpainted face, her skin darker than she imagined, with almost an Asian look. She wondered if Charlie Kim had been telling her the truth after all, that he was her father. Dressed in Stevie's jeans, his old plaid flannel shirt, and the purple cowboy boots James had given to her, Lulu found herself smiling. She had met Maggie three times as three different characters. It took a lot of confidence to do that. Maggie shouldered a lot of responsibility at the Captain Kidd House and at Ginger's studio. And Lulu knew better than anyone, her son wasn't easy to please. Saxton was a perfectionist.

"I'd love to hear about your art collection," Maggie said, trying to draw Lulu into a conversation. "Saxton mentioned you collect contemporary female artists."

"I'll invite you over for a tour," Lulu said. "Most of the collection is hanging in my apartment."

It took five days to get the results back from Ginger's tests. She had suffered a mild concussion and was prescribed a statin to prevent further transient ischemic attacks. Ginger whined like a baby that she didn't want to take pills. She was against pills. She went so far as to say that she'd rather take the falls than the pills. And she didn't want to live forever. She came up with a million reasons not to take medication. In fact, she'd never taken any kind of pills except vitamins.

"What if we grind the medicine in a special milkshake?" Maggie suggested. "You wouldn't mind that, would you? You wouldn't taste it."

Ginger grimaced and finally agreed. Maggie bought a mortar and pestle to grind the pills. Between Maggie, Spencer, and Tili, they had Ginger's milkshakes covered. And more than once Ginger actually reminded Spencer about her special milkshake when he forgot.

Before the board meeting, Maggie bought Jade lunch. She wanted to hear Jade's vision for The Captain Kidd's House and what she knew about the board members. "My father hasn't had an easy time with the board since Leonard Charney became chair," Jade said. "It seems Leonard hired a publicist and has a bucket list of things to accomplish to clear his name…of what I don't know. I'm not privy to his problems."

"How does he treat you?"

"Like an asshole. And he treats his grown kids worse. I've seen it a few times. He strong arms them."

"Your father said you're interested in working in film and television out in LA."

"Yeah, but I like working with you, Maggie. You have a wonderful spirit for improv."

"So you'll stay on for a while if I stay?"

She nodded. "I'm not ready to leave New York."

Maggie arrived prepared for Leonard Charney's boardroom.

She armed herself with a cup of tea and listened carefully throughout the meeting until it was time to discuss new business. Then she went over the report she was asked to present, describing the programs and inviting board members to come and observe. The board members visibly sighed when Magie stated that no major repairs were needed on the House at this time.

Maggie continued. "However, there are city, state, and federal grants available for programming. I'm surprised to see no record of the Kidd House ever applying for government funding in its fifty years as a nonprofit. I advise that we consider hiring a part-time development person. A good grant writer will earn back their salary in their first year. And government grants tend to grow. It's a good way to scale programs."

Leonard Charney had one very vocal advocate tooting his horn all night—a man who claimed to be a New York City history buff and whose aunt had been on the board for twenty years. Maggie decided to make a coffee date with each board member and see if she had any allies.

On the way out of the meeting, however, she and Leonard Charney shared an elevator down from the forty-eighth floor. Maggie asked about his book mentioned on the Kidd House website. He wagged his head and said that it should be finished by the end of the year. She had researched his awards for Father of the Year and Top Entrepreneur, which seemed to be granted by a religious organization that, on another page, listed him as a donor. Maggie guessed he was clueless about his brazen self-promotion and was appalled by his parting words. "I want you to cc me on every piece of email you send," he said.

FORTY

SATURDAY NIGHTS, Maggie got to know Saxton's sexual preferences, his ever-changing personas, and his various charms at full throttle. In the wee hours, she trailed along behind him and his night's chosen partner to their apartment. Maggie found a couch far from the action to sleep on and, in the morning, slipped out before they woke. When she quizzed him about the joy of sex without love, Saxton replied that sex had nothing to do with love.

"Lovemaking is a misnomer, Maggie. Sex is an art. It's about entertainment and pleasure and, hopefully, an element of delight."

"But why sex with strangers?"

"It's just about fulfilling those requirements: entertainment, pleasure, and delight."

"What about preventing sexually transmitted diseases?"

"That's a science," he assured her. "I'm always safe. I don't drink or do drugs while working, including the nights I play poker. Being responsible is an advantage."

As pleased as Maggie was that Saxton's Saturday night

performances were a financial success, she was growing tired of the late-night party scene. She didn't want to spend her savings on rent, and the job at the Kidd House wasn't enough to get her own apartment. She wanted time off to travel. Time to make her own art, and ultimately, she wanted a home. She needed to be held. She wanted love. To love and be loved.

"Is there anyone you can recommend, Saxton?"

"Recommend for what?"

"For me to love."

He took her hand in his. "Take me. I adore you."

"But we're not strangers. And you don't do love. I want love."

"Flowers," he said. "You are exceptional. You found me deposited on the side of the road and led me to shelter. Saturday nights, you deliver everything I ask—entertainment, pleasure, and delight."

"By the way," Maggie said. "How did you get the footage of me dancing solo at the men's club? I didn't tell you about it."

"I paid Mannie to look through his archives for footage. I was surprised to find you in his files. Everyone wants that footage of you. You are famous, Flowers."

"Luckily, no one knows my name or what I look like."

After their performance the following Saturday night, they took a cab to his little green house in Red Hook, Brooklyn. He set Bach's Cello Suite #1 in G Major on his record player, undressed her, and carried her to his bed. It wasn't another one of their sexualized stunts. It wasn't what she imagined sex with Saxton would be like. He was gentle. She ticked off *amusement* and *pleasure* and wondered if she could fall in love with him.

Before leaving Saxton's house the next morning, Maggie went through his storage area and found the life-size photograph of her torso graffitied with the text *Women are the real architects of society. H.B. Stowe.* She put it into a cardboard canister and mailed it to Rip when she got off the bus in downtown Brooklyn. It was a signal that the inevitable had occurred. Neither sleeping with Saxton nor Rip's girlfriend these many months interfered with her feelings for him, but their relationship had changed. Would he think the photograph brutal? Would he even see her beneath all the layers of paint? Would he toss it in the bottom of his closet like he did the crucifix as a kid? Maggie had only ever experienced Rip's kindness, so she guessed he would treat the photograph reverently and store it somewhere safe.

Three days later, on a Tuesday morning, Rip called the Captain Kidd House from Rhinebeck. As Maggie jumped out of bed and ran downstairs to answer the phone, the old wooden house trembled. At first, she assumed the homing pigeons from the roof next door had gotten into the attic again. Then, reaching for the phone, the smoke detector pierced the air. Police sirens blasted on the street.

"Hello?" she yelled.

"Maggie! A passenger jet crashed into the World Trade Center. Yamasaki's World Trade Towers were not built for this kind of impact—we studied it in structures. You need to get out of downtown now. Run north. Stay along the East River until 14th Street, then head to Union Square and up Broadway. Lulu is expecting you. 115 Central Park West, the corner of 72nd Street. Hurry."

Maggie looked out the window, mesmerized by the confetti-like debris falling from the perfectly blue sky.

"Maggie! Maggie! Can you hear me? It's Rip. The city is shutting down. Tie a cloth over your nose and mouth. Cover your head. The air is toxic. Be careful. I love you."

"I love you, too," Maggie said and set the phone down.

"Kitty," she yelled, hurrying up the two flights of stairs. She lifted the skirts to search under the beds. On the top floor, an electrical smell burned her nose and eyes. She found the cat drinking from the dripping faucet, but he ran out of an open window and under the eave. She sighed, hurried into Kidd's bedroom, and stuffed her things into the small backpack she carried everywhere. Back downstairs, she tried calling Ginger on the landline. It rang ten times before she hung up. Locking the front door, she walked two blocks north to Wall Street. Billowing black smoke poured halfway up the north Trade Tower. What if it fell? Would it stretch across the East River like another bridge to Brooklyn, or just crumble?

"Keep walking!" the police yelled through a megaphone at the crowd of cowering people. "Exit the area! Everyone, exit the area!"

Other cops bearing shields and helmets like warriors moved in formation through the street. A tank blocked the entrance to the Brooklyn Bridge. Boats of all sorts filled the East River. People pushed forward, trying to board. She quickened her pace north.

"Move on!" a cop yelled from the next corner. "Keep walking. Clear the area."

Beneath the concrete elevated F.D.R. highway, she felt safer, even as sparks seared her lungs. Remembering Rip's instructions, she found a t-shirt in her backpack and pulled it over her mouth and nose. A crowd of people stopped in the street and, looking up, pointed at the sky as a second jet crashed into the south tower. The air reverberated with a loud boom as it echoed off the skyscrapers lining the harbor. Now, a second fireball burned. Chunks of debris fell in flames as black smoke hideously covered the sky. Maggie heard cries on the street: *It's a terrorist attack!* Her eyes nearly closed against the sting, she moved more slowly, feeling her way north. She tried calling Rip, but there was no cell reception. Her legs wobbled, remembering Rip's father's plane crash when he was four. A blockade of tanks had formed at Canal Street. Police officers checked identifications. NYU students wanting access to their dorms near the Seaport argued with the cops but were forced to turn back north.

"Take cover!" a cop yelled.

Maggie shook out her baseball hat. A spark burned through it. Tossing it aside, she watched as two people holding hands fell through the sky like paper dolls. They *chose* to jump rather than burn! Maggie began coughing and pulled a long-sleeved shirt from her backpack, wound it around her head, and tied the sleeves under her chin for another layer of protection. She didn't want her hair to catch fire.

Turning down 14th Street, Union Square came into view. The sky was bright blue. She was making progress, but Union Square was barricaded. Cops with rifles stood guard. At Broadway, she watched with a group of strangers as the north tower imploded. Its monstrous plume of smoke drifted east—gritty, white, gray, and black speckled. Sirens blasted from all corners of the city. She picked up her pace again, weaving between abandoned cars and buses on Broadway. People walked silently alongside her, like concrete statues or ghosts. At 42nd Street, police with armor barricaded the street, rifles pointed. A young officer in a helmet and fatigues stopped her. After checking her driver's license, he gestured for her to move north.

She knew by the sound of it that the second tower collapsed. Her eyes teared, and she hung her head, concentrating on putting one foot in front of the other. Again, the sky to the south rained with scorching debris. She tried not to breathe. Finally reaching Central Park, the sight of green trees and grass gave her hope. Now, walking up Central Park West, she counted the street numbers, finally reaching 72nd.

"6-B," she told the doorman. "Lulu Rose."

"Your name?"

"Maggie Pierce."

"Go on up," he said.

The elevator opened onto Lulu's spacious foyer. Encased in dust, with her shirt wrapped around her head and tied beneath her chin, Maggie resembled her penitent namesake.

"Maggie! I've been so worried," Lulu whispered. "Come in. Let's undress right here and get you in the shower."

Unwinding the sleeves of the shirt from Maggie's head, Lulu dropped it in a garbage pail. She removed Maggie's backpack and set it aside. "That was quite a walk. Half the island, I think. You're safe now, Maggie."

Dust caught in her eyelashes. Her tongue felt gritty in her mouth.

"Rinse your mouth in the shower," Lulu said. "Don't swallow that dust. My word, you are covered. Shut your eyes, and I'll walk you to the bathroom."

Maggie stepped on the heel of her sneakers one by one and pushed them off. Sticking a finger in each sock, she tossed them into Lulu's garbage pail.

Guiding her down the hall, Lulu noticed a crust of white dust as if hand-drawn at Maggie's waist, neck, and ankles. Her face and hands were dusted white. "Take your time," Lulu said, adjusting the shower temperature. "I'll leave you a towel and clean clothes on the chair."

With both hands propped against the shower stall, she filled her mouth with water and spit. She blew her nose, wiped her eyes, and scraped the grit out of her ears. Soapy, warm water loosened the stuff in her hair, and it felt sharp beneath her feet. *Is it glass, concrete, plastic, metal? Or shards of human bone? How did it so thoroughly penetrate the nooks and crannies of my flesh?* The creepy feeling reminded her of the mysterious blood that appeared on her palm and forehead as she strolled through Rhinebeck with Rip. A new reality was beginning to sink in: two passenger jets exploded like bombs into the Trade Towers! It was a planned attack. Is this war?

Scrubbed clean, Maggie dressed in a pair of sweatpants and a long-sleeved t-shirt. She wrapped her hair in a towel and found her way to the living room. Curled up on the sofa, she faced the green of Central Park. The one-eyed cat at the Kidd House never once curled in her lap or rubbed against her legs. She doubted he hunkered down somewhere safe but was on the run and somehow would probably survive the destruction.

Lulu placed a glass of water on the coffee table. "You must be dehydrated," she said. "Were you able to call your mother to let her know you were coming here? And Carol's parents?"

Maggie shook her head.

"My landline is still working. I'll call Gertrude and ask her to pass on the news that you are safe. Saxton is in Brooklyn, and Kermit had a nine o'clock appointment at the gallery. He'll walk over when he feels up to it."

Maggie rested her head on the back of the sofa and shut her eyes. Lulu placed a blanket over her lap just as Gertrude and Roland had on the day of Rip's tennis tournament. Lulu's kindness overwhelmed Maggie. She was kind when Ginger needed help and kind the night she arrived with Saxton, her torso graffitied and face painted. Saxton, the melodramatic bad boy with the camera, the schemer for cash and sexual escapades, always on the prowl for the next cultural happening, always folding his winnings into his next game. Saxton was kind, too. Last Saturday night, after stripping the artifice from her body in some stranger's shower, Maggie found Saxton asleep with his lover and slipped beneath their covers. In the morning, the three were a tangle of limbs like sleeping children. Saxton's soft side soothed her, his recitations charmed. She welcomed his affection. Their casual goodbye on a Village sidewalk Sunday morning got approval from an elderly woman who commented: *that was a nice kiss.*

"After you rest," Lulu said. "I'll show you my collection of paintings. I have a very small Artemisia Gentileschi, one of her only paintings not in a museum, a gift from Kermit. A Georgia O'Keeffe. Frida Kahlo. Louise Bourgeois, Barbara Kruger, Jenny Holzer, Yayoi Kusama, Judy Chicago, Julie Mehretu… Yoko Ono… Mickalene Thomas… Mira Dancy… Kiki Smith."

The women's names blurred with the sirens on Central Park West. The silhouettes of humans holding hands continued to fall behind Maggie's closed eyelids. She imagined the endless rush of gravity pulling her down, but she never hit the earth. Maggie lived, yet how many thousands died? In her rush uptown to reach Lulu's apartment, a tiny piece of paper caught on her sleeve with the typed words: soon there is. *Soon what is*, she wondered? Did someone in one of the towers sit at their computer and write of their imminent death? What exactly happened to the space 1,368 feet up in the sky where Philippe Petit walked? Does it exist if we can't pinpoint it?

Lulu sat beside Maggie on the sofa and began to chant in slow, undulating Hebrew. Maggie recognized it as the Kaddish, the prayer for the dead she had learned while studying for her bat mitzvah. Lefty and Stevie were still alive then, and for Maggie, the Kaddish simply signaled that the end of the service was near. Now, sorrow and death bloomed in her gut. She began to hum the melody, her voice mixing with Lulu's like a confluence of streams, and the slow, mournful prayer amplified to the sonorous vibration of a High Holy Day service. When the last long notes of A-MEN fell to a hush, they opened their eyes. Kermit sat across from them, tears streaking his face. He dabbed his eyes with a white handkerchief as he had many, many times before. Love and war were great bleeding wounds. Maggie was so grateful to Rip for getting her out of downtown and for the refuge of Lulu and Kermit's home. And she was grateful that none of them judged poorly of her for falling for the man in the long black coat.

The End

ACKNOWLEDGMENTS

Enormous thanks goes to my publisher, Stephanie Larkin, who offered me a three book contract, and for her creation of the new imprint Emperor Books for award winning writers. I'd also like to thank her assistant Denise Reichert, editor Katherine Abraham and the rest of the Red Penguin team. My deepest gratitude goes to photographer Sergio Purtell and graphic designer Melanie Roberts for this exquisite book cover. I'm truly grateful for the enthusiasm of my first readers of *Tinker Street*— June Crane, Judy Jablon, Dianne Kane, Amy Mereson, and especially to Ellen Busch whose generosity and editorial expertise were invaluable.

This book could not have been written without the New York City arts and cultural organizations where I honed my artistic visions, especially The Lee Strasberg Theatre and Film Institute and the Anne Frank Center. I'd like to publicly thank my mentors Margarete Phillips, Martha LeValley and Jo McNeil whose spirits are alive in this book; and to Sheri Andrews, Janet Neuhauser, Luz Minerva Muniz and Nancy Wu Houk for journeying with me and Maggie these last two years. A big shout out also goes to the eight-year-old I met jumping rope in front of my Red Hook, Brooklyn house, Mercedes Cabbagestalk, who years later changed my life when she asked if she could call me mom. Thanks to my sons—Isaac, Henry and Will—who opened up my world as they discovered theirs. Finally, thanks to my husband Paul Glovinsky for everything.

ABOUT THE AUTHOR

Maureen McNeil is an author, artist and activist from the Pacific Northwest living in Brooklyn and the Hudson Valley. Her previous books include *Anna Magdalena* (2022); *Wild Blueberries* (2022); *Dear Red: The Lost Diary of Marilyn Monroe, A Work of Fiction* (2017); *Red Hook Stories* (2008); and *Red Hook Poems* (1985). She was a finalist for the 2021 Tiferet Fiction Prize and won second place for the 2021 Barry Lopez Nonfiction Award. McNeil has lectured, designed and taught writing workshops in partnership with the Anne Frank Center, PEN America Prison Program, Prison Public Memory Project, Yad Vashem, United Nations, the Morgan Library, Skidmore College and Woodstock Day School.